"I've never wanted a woman the way I want you.

"Come here," he commanded when she breezed past the four-poster. His delft-blue eyes were smoldering with passion.

"Not on your life," she teased, but when he reached out and took hold of her wrist, she was forced to spin around and face the determined set of his jaw. Her wet hair dangled in glistening ebony ringlets around her flushed face as he roughly pulled her down on the bed.

"You're no gentleman, Senator Daniels." She laughed as she fell against him.

"And you love it." His fingers toyed with the buttons of her sweater. "Someone should teach you a lesson, you know."

"And you're applying for the job?"

"I've got it."

Dear Reader:

Nora Roberts, Tracy Sinclair, Jeanne Stephens, Carole Halston, Linda Howard. Are these authors familiar to you? We hope so, because they are just a few of our most popular authors who publish with Silhouette Special Edition each and every month. And the Special Edition list is changing to include new writers with fresh stories. It has been said that discovering a new author is like making a new friend. So during these next few months, be sure to look for books by Sandi Shane, Dorothy Glenn and other authors who have just written their first and second Special Editions, stories we hope you enjoy.

Choosing which Special Editions to publish each month is a pleasurable task, but not an easy one. We look for stories that are sophisticated, sensuous, touching, and great love stories, as well. These are the elements that make Silhouette Special Editions more romantic... and unique.

So we hope you'll find this Silhouette Special Edition just that—*Special*—and that the story finds a special place in your heart.

The Editors at Silhouette

SERL-7/85

LISA JACKSON
Midnight Sun

Silhouette Special Edition

Published by Silhouette Books New York

America's Publisher of Contemporary Romance

To the two and only,
Cousin Dave and Cousin Les

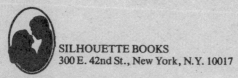

SILHOUETTE BOOKS
300 E. 42nd St., New York, N.Y. 10017

Copyright © 1985 by Lisa Jackson

Distributed by Pocket Books

ISBN: 0-373-09264-4

First Silhouette Books printing September 1985

10 9 8 7 6 5 4 3 2 1

America's Publisher of Contemporary Romance

Printed in the U.S.A.

Books by Lisa Jackson

Silhouette Intimate Moments

Dark Side of the Moon #39
Gypsy Wind #79

Silhouette Special Editions

A Twist of Fate #118
The Shadow of Time #180
Tears of Pride #194
Pirate's Gold #215
A Dangerous Precedent #233
Innocent by Association #244
Midnight Sun #264

LISA JACKSON

was raised in Molalla, Oregon, and now lives with her husband, Mark, and her two sons in a suburb of Portland. Lisa and her sister, Natalie Bishop, who is also a Silhouette author, live within earshot of each other and do all their work in Natalie's basement.

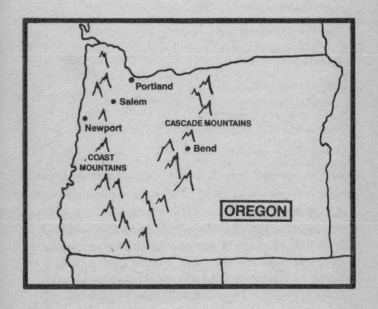

Chapter One

Holding her head proudly, Ashley walked into the room and gave no outward sign of her flagging confidence. Her elegant features were emotionless and the regal tilt of her chin didn't falter. The only signs of the emotional turmoil which stole her sleep were the deep blue smudges beneath her eyes.

She was reminded of vultures circling over carrion as she stepped into the law offices of McMichaels and Lee. Alan McMichaels held the chair for her, and as she took her seat between her cousin Claud and Aunt Beatrice, Ashley could feel the cool disdain in the pinched, white faces of the five people seated near the oiled oak desk.

Claud's rust-colored eyebrows had raised in mild surprise when she entered the room, but he said nothing.

Aunt Beatrice nodded stiffly and then turned her pale gold eyes back on the attorney.

The family had never been particularly close. Or, at least, Ashley had never felt the kinship with her father's relatives that some families share.

Today was no exception. Her father's death hadn't brought the family together. If anything, the family, whose members each owned a small piece of Stephens Timber Corporation, seemed more fragmented than ever.

Though the room was spacious and decorated in opulent tones of cobalt blue and brown, the atmosphere within the brushed plaster walls was awkward and confining. Tension, like an invisible electric current, charged the air.

Alan McMichaels took a seat at the modern desk. Behind his chair, through a large, plate glass window, was an expansive view of the West Hills of Portland. The fir-laden slopes, still a rich forest green in winter, were covered with expensive, turn-of-the-century homes that overlooked the city. In the distance, spanning two high ridges, was the Vista Bridge. Its elegant gray arch was just visible in the gentle morning fog that had settled upon the city.

The lean attorney with the silver hair and black eyebrows cleared his throat and caught everyone's attention. "As you know, we're here for the reading of Lazarus Stephens's will. Please hold your comments until I've read the entire document. When I'm finished, I'll answer all of your questions."

McMichaels adjusted his reading glasses and picked up the neatly typed document. A claustrophobic feeling took hold of Ashley and wouldn't let go. The tears she had shed for her father were dry and the only thing she felt was a deep, inexplicable loneliness. She and her father had never been close, but she felt as if a part of her had died with him.

Despite the unspoken accusations of the other people in the room, Ashley met each questioning gaze with the cool serenity of her intelligent green eyes. Her blue-black hair was coiled neatly at the nape of her neck in a tight knot of ebony silk, and she was dressed expensively in a dark blue suit of understated elegance.

Ashley understood the condemning looks from her father's family. With very few exceptions the relatives of Lazarus Stephens didn't approve of Ashley and made no bones about it. Ashley imagined that they had all been secretly pleased when they had learned of the falling-out between Lazarus and his headstrong, spoiled daughter. Aunts, uncles and cousins alike treated her like an outsider.

Ignoring the surreptitious glances being cast in her direction, Ashley folded her hands in her lap and stared calmly at the silver-haired, bespectacled man sitting directly across the desk from her. Alan McMichaels was addressing everyone in the room, but Ashley was left with the distinct impression that he was singling her out.

"I, Lazarus J. Stephens of Portland, Oregon, do make, publish and declare my Last Will and Testament, revoking all previous Wills and Codicils...." Ashley listened to her father's attorney, and her wide green eyes showed no sign of emotion as the reading of the will progressed. Though she remained outwardly calm, her stomach was tied into several painful knots while the small bequests were made to each of Lazarus Stephens's closest friends and relatives.

McMichaels had insisted that Ashley attend the reading of her father's will, although she didn't understand why. Unless, of course, it was her father's wish that she listen in humiliation while Lazarus publicly announced for the last time that he had disinherited his only child.

She paled at the memory of the violent scene that had resulted in the rift separating them. Vividly she could recall the rage that had colored his cheeks, the vicious accusations that had claimed she had "sold out" and betrayed him, and the look of utter disdain and disappointment in his faded blue eyes.

Over the years, the gap between father and daughter had narrowed, but never had that one, horrible scene been forgotten. Though Ashley had chosen to ignore the rumors about her father and his business practices, she hadn't been immune to the malicious gossip that seemed to spread like wildfire whenever his name was mentioned in private conversation.

Alan McMichaels cleared his throat and his dark eyes locked with Ashley's for an instant. "...my nephew Claud," McMichaels continued. In her peripheral vision Ashley saw Claud lean forward and noticed that his anxious fingers ran nervously along the edge of the polished desk as he stared expectantly at the attorney. "...I bequeath the sum of one hundred thousand dollars."

Claud's self-assured smile, hidden partially by a thick, rust-colored mustache, wavered slightly as McMichaels paused. Claud's nervous eyes darted from McMichaels to Ashley and back again.

"I give, devise and bequeath all of the residue of my estate unto my only child, Ashley Stephens Jennings, to be hers absolutely."

Ashley's heart dropped and her face drained of all color. She was forced to close her eyes for a second as she digested the intent of her father's will. *He had forgiven her.* But his stubborn pride hadn't allowed Lazarus to confront his daughter. Her fingers clenched together. Hot tears of grief burned in her eyes as she accepted her father's final forgiveness.

McMichaels had continued reading, but the words were a muffled sound in Ashley's private world of grief. She couldn't look into the eyes of the startled family members.

"Wait a minute—" Claud started to interrupt, but a killing stare from Alan McMichaels forestalled any further comment from Ashley's cousin. Claud sent Ashley a stricken look bordering on hatred.

McMichaels's voice droned on for a few minutes until he finally tapped the neatly typed sheets of white paper on the tabletop and smiled. "That's it. If you have any questions—"

The voices around the table started to buzz, and Ashley felt the eyes of distant relatives bore into her. Pieces of the whispered conversation drifted to her ears.

"I never suspected..."

"Didn't Uncle Laz cut her off?"

"I thought so. Something about an affair with that Trevor Daniels, you know, the one running for the senatorial seat this fall."

"How could she? And with that man! He was accused of taking a bribe last summer sometime. The charges didn't stick, but if you ask me, he paid somebody off to save his neck! Trevor Daniels isn't a man to trust or get involved with!"

"Daniels swore he'd break Lazarus, you know. He always blamed Lazarus for his father's disappearance. If you ask me, Trevor Daniels's father...what was his name? Robert—that's right. I'll bet that Robert Daniels just took off with another woman...."

Ashley lifted her chin fractionally and leveled cool green eyes on the members of her father's family. She was accustomed to the pain of gossip and she managed to let her poise lift her above the insulting speculation being whispered just loud enough for her to hear. Pushing her chair away from the desk, Ashley stood and started toward the door.

Claud was leaning over McMichaels's desk, his ruddy complexion redder than usual. Though he was whispering, Ashley was well aware of what he was threatening. Claud considered himself next in line for control of the

Stephens timber empire. No doubt cousin Claud was already devising ways of contesting the will.

Alan McMichaels noticed that Ashley was leaving, and he broke off his conversation with Claud in order to talk to her. He held up his palm to get her attention. "Ms Jennings—please. If you could stay for a few more minutes. There are a few matters I'd like to discuss with you."

Managing a frail smile, Ashley nodded before smoothing her skirt and walking across the room to stand near the windows. She felt, rather than saw, the hateful glances cast at her back.

Though Ashley's gaze studied the view from the eighth floor of the building, she didn't notice the tall spire of a Gothic church steeple in the foreground or the fact that the fog had begun to lift, promising a cold, but clear, November day. Her thoughts rested on her father and the horrible fight that had torn them apart.

It had taken place in the spacious library of Lazarus's Tudor home on Palatine Hill. "How could you?" Lazarus had shouted, his shock and rage white-hot when he had discovered that the man Ashley had been seeing all summer was the son of Robert Daniels, the man who had been Lazarus's rival before his mysterious disappearance not two years earlier. Lazarus's faded blue eyes had sparked vengeful fire, and his shoulders had slumped in defeat. Nothing Ashley could have done would have wounded him more.

When she had tried to explain that she loved Trevor and planned to marry him, her father had laughed.

"Marry a Daniels? Damn it, Ashley, I thought you had more brains than that!" Lazarus had shaken his graying head. "What do you think he wants from you? Love?" When Lazarus read the expectant light in her eyes, he had spit angrily into the fire. "He's using you, don't you see? He's after the timber company, for Christ's sake! He's on some personal vendetta against me. Wake up girl. Trevor Daniels doesn't care a damn about you."

When Ashley had staunchly refused to stop seeing Trevor, Lazarus had slapped his open palm on the table and threatened to disinherit her. Angrily, she had told him to do just that and had stomped out of the room, out of his house and out of her father's life. Determined that she was right, Ashley had been hell-bent to prove him wrong.

It had been an impossible task. Lazarus had been correct about Trevor and his motives all along. At the vividly painful memory, Ashley sighed and ran her fingers along the cool window ledge. One again tears, bitter and deceitful, threatened to spill.

"Ashley, could I have a word with you? It will only take a few minutes."

She turned to face her father's attorney and noticed that the room was empty. "First, let me tell you I'm sorry about your father." She nodded, accepting his condolences and somehow holding on to her frail composure. "And that I hope you'll continue to retain the services of McMichaels and Lee for yourself as well as the business." Once again she nodded, encouraging him to get to the point.

"You must realize that, with your father's bequest, you own a large majority of the stock of Stephens Timber. It's within your power to run the company or hire someone else—"

"Mr. McMichaels," Ashley interrupted, finally able to collect her scattered thoughts. "Right now, I don't think I'm qualified to run the company myself."

"But your father thought you could. Don't you have a degree in business administration?"

"A master's—"

"And didn't you work for the corporation?"

"Years ago—during the summers between school terms. But the industry has changed a lot in the last eight years," she protested.

"Your father seemed to think that you had a real knack for handling the executive end of Stephens Timber."

"Did he?" Ashley shook her head in confusion. Why hadn't her father been able to tell her what McMichaels was repeating? "I think we should leave things just as they are for the time being. It was my understanding that Claud had been managing the day-to-day transactions for all practical purposes. My father was in semiretirement."

"That's right."

Ashley forced herself to think clearly. The strain of the past few days had been exhausting, but she couldn't ignore her responsibilities. "So, until I know a little more about the business, and until my teaching contract is fulfilled, I'll have to rely on Claud. The only thing I'll require for the present is an audit of the company books and monthly financial statements. I'll talk to Claud and ask him to continue to stay on as general manager of the corporation, at least temporarily.''

McMichaels stuffed his hands into his pockets and appeared uneasy.

"Is there a problem with that?''

The attorney frowned, seemed about to say something and thought better of it. "No, I suppose not. You can do whatever you like.''

"I know about the company's reputation,'' she assured the surprised lawyer. "I haven't lived my life with my head in the sand. I expect that Claud will see to it that anything Stephens Timber does is strictly legal. Advising him will be your job.''

McMichaels smiled. Relief was evident on his tanned features. "Good.''

Ashley managed a thin smile. It was the first since the news of her father's heart attack. "Whether I like it or not, I've got a teaching contract that doesn't expire until June fifteenth. I'll talk to the administration and explain the situation, and if the community college can find a substitute for next term, I'll consider moving back to Portland and working with Claud.''

"I think that would be wise,'' McMichaels agreed. He touched her shoulder in a consoling gesture. "You're a very wealthy woman, now, Ashley. You'll have to be careful. People will be out to take advantage of you.''

"Only if I give them the chance,'' she replied. Ashley spoke a few more minutes with her father's attorney and left his office with the disturbing feeling that something was on Alan McMichaels's mind. She shook off the uncomfortable sensation and reasoned that the lawyer wanted to give her a little more time to deal with her grief before hoisting any corporate problems onto her shoulders.

Once in the elevator, Ashley was alone. She closed her eyes and moved her head from side to side, hoping to relieve some of the tension in her shoulders.

Pushing through the glass doors of the building housing the firm of McMichaels and Lee, Ashley stepped into the subdued winter sunlight. A slight breeze caught in her hair and chilled her to the bone. She had just started down the short flight of steps to the street when Claud accosted her. Ashley braced herself for the confrontation that was sure to come. Ever since her falling out with her father, Claud had been groomed to inherit the presidency of Stephens Timber. No doubt his feathers were more than slightly ruffled.

"You knew about the change in the will, didn't you?" he charged, falling into step with her.

"Of course not."

"I don't understand it—"

"Neither do I. Not really, but the fact is that father left the company to me." When she reached her car, she turned to face her cousin. "Look, Claud, I know this must be a shock and disappointment to you. The thing of it is that I'd like you to continue to run the corporation just as you did for Dad, but you'll have to report to me. I've told Alan exactly what I expect from you."

Claud tugged uneasily on his mustache. His dark eyes bored into hers. "You won't interfere?"

"Of course I will—*if* I think you're doing an inadequate job. The next few days I'll be at the corporate offices, looking over your shoulder. We can get any of the more pressing problems ironed out then. I want to know everything that happens to Stephens Timber Corporation."

"Then you're moving to Portland?" Claud asked, shifting from one foot to the other. He pulled at the knotted silk tie and found it difficult to look Ashley in the eye.

"Maybe after spring break, if the school administration can replace me. I expect you to send me reports and call me if you have a problem."

"I think I will handle everything," Claud stated with his cocky self-assurance. "Your old man didn't bother to oversee what I was doing."

"Well I am," Ashley stated, her eyes glittering with determination. "Because now it's my reputation on the line."

"Don't tell me you believed all those rumors."

"Gossip is a cheap sort of entertainment for idle minds. What I believe happened in the past doesn't matter. But, from here on in, we keep our corporate nose clean. Stephens Timber can't afford any more bad press." She added emphasis to her words by tapping her fingers on the hood of her car.

Claud grinned broadly. He reassessed his first cousin and his eyes slid appreciatively down her slender body.

Ashley Jennings was a woman with class. It was too damn bad she just happened to be Lazarus Stephens's daughter. "We do have one particular problem," Claud speculated aloud.

"What's that?" Ashley had pulled the keys from her purse and her hand was poised over the handle of the car door. She and Claud had never gotten along, but because of the situation, she was forced to trust him, if only temporarily.

"Trevor Daniels."

"Why is he a problem?" Ashley looked unperturbed and gave no indication of her suddenly racing pulse. After eight years of living with the truth, she was able to react calmly whenever Trevor's name was mentioned.

"If he gets the senatorial seat in the fall, he'll put us out of business."

"I don't see how that's possible, Claud." She turned to face her cousin. Her green eyes were still clear and hid the fact that her heart was pounding erratically.

"He's always been out to get the family. You, as well as anyone, should know that," Claud stated.

Ashley felt her body stiffen, but she promised herself not to let Claud's insensitive remarks affect her.

She straightened before crossing her arms over her chest and leaning on her sporty BMW. "Trevor's family, as well as ours, is involved in the timber business. We're competitors—that's all. There's no way he would be able to 'put us out of business.'"

Claud's hands were spread open at his sides. "But you know how he is—he's trying to get the government to make all the forests into designated wilderness areas. If he gets elected—"

"He'll try harder." Ashley's small hands pushed her away from the car. "But not to the point that it would destroy the timber industry. If he did that, Claud, he'd not only thwart his own family's business, but he'd also put a lot of his constituents back in the unemployment lines. He's too smart to do anything of the sort."

"I can't figure it out," Claud said, his eyes narrowing suspiciously.

"What?"

"Why the hell you still stick up for that bastard!"

Ashley raised an elegant eyebrow and smiled confidently. "What happened between Trevor and me has nothing to do with Stephens Timber."

"Like hell! When are you going to face the fact that the bastard used you, Ashley? And all for a chance at the timber company. He thought you would inherit it all, didn't he? And then, when your father cut you off, he split! Swell guy."

"There's no reason to discuss this any further," Ashley replied, her cheeks beginning to burn.

"Just remember that he's out to get Stephens Timber," Claud warned. "He still thinks Lazarus had something to do with his father's disappearance."

Ashley managed to smile sweetly despite the fact that her blood had turned cold. "And just remember who signs your paycheck."

"You need me," Claud reminded her.

"Of course I do, and I'd hate to lose your expertise at managing the company. But that's all I expect from you, and I don't need any lectures about my personal life." Her dark brows arched over determined green eyes.

At that moment Claud understood that tangling with his beautiful cousin would be more difficult than he had imagined. It looked as if, after all, Ashley had inherited more than the timber fortune; she also had received some of her father's resolve. Claud raised his hands in mock surrender. "All right. Just be careful, Ashley. It wouldn't surprise me a bit if Trevor Daniels suddenly started paying a lot of attention to you. You can't trust him."

"I think I can deal with Trevor," Ashley responded with more confidence than she felt. When Claud finally left her alone, she slid into the car, placed her hands on the steering wheel and let the bitter tears of pain slide down her face.

Trevor opened a weary eye. As he lifted his head the weight of the hangover hit him like a ton of bricks. He was still seated in the leather recliner by the fireplace, and his muscles were cramped from the awkward position and the cold morning air. A half-full glass of Scotch, now stale, sat on the small table near his chair next to the newspaper article that had been the impetus for his uncharacteristic binge. The bold headlines were still visible, but the rest of the article was smeared from the liquor that had slopped over the rim of the glass and spilled onto the newsprint.

Running a tired hand over the stubble on his chin, Trevor stretched and cursed himself for his own lack of control. How many drinks had he consumed while locked in memories of the past—four, five? He couldn't remember. The last time he had been so drunk was the night of Ashley's betrayal....

Of their own accord, his vibrant blue eyes returned to the headline: TIMBER BARON DEAD AT 70. The paper was three days old.

"You bastard," Trevor murmured before wadding the newspaper and tossing it into the smoldering remains of the fire. The paper ignited and was instantly consumed by hungry flames.

The first gray light of dawn was already shadowing the spacious den with the promise of another cold November morning. With an effort, Trevor pulled himself out of the chair and ran his fingers through his thick chestnut hair. His mouth tasted rancid and he wondered if it was from too much liquor, too little sleep or the painful memories of Ashley. The article about the death of Ashley's father, Lazarus Stephens, had conjured up all the old pain again—the pain Trevor had promised to put behind him.

Maybe it was impossible. Perhaps Ashley's life and his were entwined irrevocably by the sins of their fathers. Whatever the reason, Trevor had difficulty dismissing the image of her shining black hair and intriguing sea-green eyes.

Trevor rubbed his temple as he walked to the window and let his eyes wander outside the house, past the landscaped lawns and through the denuded trees of the estate his father had purchased. He leaned against the windowsill and considered the unlikely course of events that would never allow him to be free of her.

The feud between the two timber families had been long, ruthless and bloody. Rumor had it that sometime before the Korean War, the partners, who owned a small Oregon logging firm, had become embroiled in such a vicious argument that they had parted ways, each vowing to destroy the other. The stories varied slightly but all seemed to agree that the cause of the dispute was graft. Robert Daniels had supposedly caught Lazarus Stephens skimming off company profits for personal use.

The result of the breakup was that Stephens Timber Corporation and Daniels Logging Company became bitter enemies within the Oregon timber industry.

Trevor didn't know how many of the rumors that had circulated scandalously over the past forty years were true and how many were fictitious. But he was certain of one thing: Lazarus Stephens had been involved in the disappearance of Trevor's father, Robert Daniels.

Ten years before, when Robert had disappeared, Trevor had sworn that not only would he avenge his father, but he would personally see to it that the people responsible for the crime would be punished. But he had been deterred by his feelings for Ashley.

What had happened to Robert Daniels, after he was last seen leaving the dinner meeting with a lobbyist from Washington, D.C., remained a mystery. And now Lazarus Stephens, Ashley's father, the one man who knew the answer, was dead.

Ashley. Just the thought of her innocent eyes and enigmatic smile touched a traitorous part of Trevor's soul. He squeezed his eyes tightly shut, as if he could physically deny the vivid image of her elegant face surrounded by glossy ebony curls.

Thinking of Ashley and her betrayal still made him clench his teeth together in frustration, and he silently cursed himself for caring. Hadn't she shown her true colors? Hadn't she tossed him out of her life and married another man?

Trevor had been blind to her faults and had let his feelings for her manipulate him. But now the tables had turned; if the senatorial race ended in his favor, he would personally see to it that all the suspicious dealings of Stephens Timber were investigated and halted.

His blue eyes narrowed as he stared past the leafless trees to the silvery waters of the Willamette River. A soft morning fog clung tenaciously to the shoreline.

What if Ashley inherited Lazarus's share of Stephens Timber Corporation? What if all those rumors that her father disinherited her were only idle speculation? What if Ashley was now the woman in charge of the corporation Trevor had vowed to destroy?

His headache began to pound furiously just as the telephone rang. Trevor Daniels was jerked back to the present and the most pressing problem of the day: winning the election in the fall.

Chapter Two

During the next few weeks, Ashley's impatience with her cousin mounted with the passing of each day, and her concern for Stephens Timber drew her attention away from Trevor and his candidacy in the May primary. Trevor's face was continually in the news and Ashley was glad for the distraction of the timber company. It helped her keep the memories of the love she had shared with him pushed into a dark corner of her mind.

Between studying the reports that Claud had grudgingly begun to send her and instructing her classes, Ashley barely had a moment to herself. When she was able to find a few minutes to relax, her thoughts would invariably return to Trevor and the few blissful months they had shared together nearly eight years ago.

Now she owned the lion's share of the company Trevor had vowed to destroy.

"Oh, stop it," she admonished as she sat at the cluttered kitchen table in her small apartment near the campus. "You're beginning to sound as paranoid as Claud." At the mention of her shifty cousin's name, Ashley frowned. It didn't take a supersleuth to realize that Claud was up to something, but Ashley didn't know exactly what. The information he had been sending concerning the timber company was sketchy at best. Ashley had the uneasy feeling that Claud was deliberately trying to hide something from her.

The first report from Claud hadn't been as encompassing as Ashley had hoped, but when she had asked her cousin for a more lengthy audit of the books of Stephens Timber, Claud had been reluctant to send it to her.

"Don't worry yourself," he had soothed when she had called him and demanded more complete information. "You've got more than you can handle with your teaching job. Besides which, I've got everything under control up here."

"That's not the issue, Claud. I need the reports," Ashley had insisted.

"Then you'd better come up and look at them," Claud had growled, losing his veneer of civility. "I don't like sending out that kind of information. Right now we've got a shortage of personnel in the bookkeeping department, and I wouldn't want to trust the post office to get the reports to you, even if we were able to put them together."

"You're stalling, Claud," she had responded. "Get the reports together and send them in tomorrow's mail, or I just might take you up on your offer and come up to Portland to see for myself just how well you've 'got everything under control.'"

"Look, Ashley, I don't need a keeper!"

Ashley had begun to worry in earnest.

"And Claud?"

"What?"

"For God's sake, hire the help you need in accounting!"

Claud's reply had been a disgusted snort, indicating all too well what he thought about Ashley's interference in what he considered his domain.

Claud's reluctance had been all the reason she needed to talk to the school administration about getting out of her teaching contract. Within a week, the administration had found a suitable replacement to take over her classes for the rest of the school year. All she had to do was finish the term, and that task was nearly accomplished. Christmas vacation started next week.

At that thought, Ashley quit thinking about her cousin and let her gaze return to the untidy stack of papers sitting on the table. As she started grading the tests, she listened to a local news channel on the television.

She was frowning at a particularly bad answer to one of her questions and sipping coffee when news of an accident involving Trevor was announced by the even-featured anchorman.

Ashley almost spilled her coffee, her throat constricted in fear and her eyes snapped upward to stare at the small television situated on the kitchen counter. She had left it on for background noise, but at the sound of Trevor's name, all of her attention became riveted to the set.

"...Trevor Daniels was rushed to Andrews Hospital in Salem when the car he was driving slid off the road, broke through the guardrail and rolled down an embankment...." The screen flashed from the earnest reporter to the site of the accident and the twisted wreckage of Trevor's car.

Ashley's stomach knotted and nausea rose in her throat. "Dear God," she whispered, placing her hand protectively over her heart. Her blood ran as cold as the clear December night. The pencil she had been holding over a stack of papers dropped unobserved onto the table as she concentrated on what the wavy-haired reporter was saying.

"Reports have varied as to the cause of the accident," the reporter, once again on the screen, told the viewing audience. "Police are investigating the site, but as yet have not confirmed the rumors of foul play. Mr. Daniels remains in serious, but stable condition."

"No," Ashley murmured, at the fleeting thoughts of Trevor and the love they had shared. Absently, she removed her reading glasses, rubbed her temples and stared at the screen. When she found the strength to move, she pushed her chair away from the table and some coffee spilled onto the tests. She didn't notice.

Without considering her motives, she dialed operator assistance and was given the number of Andrews Hospital. Her fingers were trembling when she punched out the number for the hospital in Salem. After several rings, a member of the staff answered and told her politely, but firmly, that Mr. Daniels was taking no calls and seeing no visitors.

Ashley replaced the receiver and slumped against the wall. What was happening? Within the course of three weeks her father had suffered a fatal heart attack, she had inherited the company and now, Trevor Daniels, the only man she had ever loved, had nearly been killed. The reporter had glossed over the mention of foul play; certainly no one would want to harm Trevor....

Get a hold of yourself, she warned. *He doesn't care for you—never did. Nothing will ever change that.*

She continued to listen to the news program, hoping that a later bulletin would give her an update on Trevor's condition. After wiping the table, she poured herself a fresh cup of coffee and tried to concentrate on the test papers she had been grading. The task was impossible.

Teasing thoughts of Trevor, provocative images of a younger, more carefree time, continued to assail her. She remembered the first time she had seen him more than eight years before. She had been immediately attracted by his flash of a rakish smile, and his lean, well-muscled body. But it was his eyes that had caught her attention and captured her heart. They were a brilliant shade of blue and challenged her silently. The hint of amusement in their clear depths had touched a very intimate part of her—and had never let go. Those damned blue eyes seemed to look through her sophisticated facade and bore into her soul and they had dared her to seduce him....

With a start, she dragged herself back to the present. "Don't brood about what might have been," she told herself, though her stomach had knotted painfully.

If she could just get through the next few days, she would have time to herself and by that time she would know more about Trevor's accident.

"No one is allowed to visit Mr. Daniels," the rotund nurse insisted upon Ashley's inquiry. The large woman was standing behind the glass enclosure of the hospital reception area and had only looked up from her paperwork when Ashley had inquired about Trevor.

"But I'm a personal friend," Ashley stated with a patient smile. She hadn't spent the last two hours in the car to be thwarted by hospital politics.

"It wouldn't matter if you were his mother," the strict nurse replied, glancing up from the chart she had been studying. In the past two days she had dismissed five reporters, seven photographers and about fifteen "personal friends" of the famous man lying in room 214. Security in the hospital had been increased due to the celebrity of Trevor Daniels. The sooner Mr. Daniels was out of the hospital, the better, for staff and patient alike.

The nurse, whose name tag indicated that she was Janelle Wilkes, smiled warmly. "I'm sorry, Ms—"

"Jennings. Ashley Jennings," Ashley supplied.

"I'll tell Mr. Daniels that you were by."

"I'd appreciate it," Ashley retorted, sneaking a longing look down the corridors of the building. If she could only have a quick glimpse of Trevor—just enough to ease her mind, so that she would be convinced that he was indeed recuperating and on the road to recovery.

She left the hospital in frustration, after giving the nurse her name and telephone number.

Ashley didn't really expect Trevor to call, and she wasn't disappointed. In the next few days, while school was ending for the holidays, Ashley had been in and out of her apartment, but either Trevor hadn't called, or she had missed him. She suspected that the would-be senator had received her message and promptly tossed it in the trash.

She told herself that she would never try to contact him again.

His wound had healed to the point where he could take charge of his life again, and Trevor Daniels intended to start this morning. Ignoring the warnings from his concerned campaign manager, Trevor hoisted his suitcase from the closet and tossed it carelessly onto the bed.

He couldn't wait to break away from Portland. His plan was simple. All he needed was a few hours alone with Ashley.

Hiding a grimace of pain, Trevor withdrew a faded pair of jeans from the closet and stuffed them into the open canvas bag. Determination was evident in the knit of his thick, dark brows and the hard angle of his jaw.

Everett Woodward, wearing an expression of disapproval on his round face, walked into the room and silently observed Trevor's deliberate movements. He sipped his second drink patiently while he watched Trevor fill the bag with casual clothes. It was obvious that Trevor had a purpose in mind, a purpose he hadn't confided to his campaign manager. Everett took a chair near the window in the master suite of Trevor's home. The would-be senator had noticed his entrance, but chose to ignore it. Everett frowned into his drink, silently plotting his line of reasoning to deter Trevor from making the worst political decision of his life. The damned thing of it was that Trevor had never thought rationally whenever Ashley Stephens was involved. And this time, Ashley was involved. Everett knew it.

"You know that I think you're making a big mistake," Everett ventured, stealing a quick glance through the window at the threatening sky. The chill of December seeped through the panes. There was the promise of snow in the air.

"So what else is new?" Trevor retorted with no trace of humor. He threw a bulky ski sweater into the bag before zipping it closed and eyeing his uneasy companion. "You always think I'm making mistakes."

"You're a gambler," Everett pointed out with a frown. "Gambling and politics don't mix."

"I can't argue with that." Trevor reached for his jacket and tried to change the course of the conversation. "I thought you were downstairs going over political strategy or something of the sort."

Everett avoided the trap and concentrated on the subject at hand. "We're not talking about some obscure issue here," Everett reminded the lean, angry man staring at him from across the room. "Your entire political future is on the line—everything you've worked for. The way I see it, this is too big a risk to take."

Trevor's square jaw tightened and the thin lines around his eyes became more distinct as his gaze hardened. "The way *I* see it, I don't have much of a choice." The small red scar on his cheek seemed to emphasize his words.

"You're not thinking clearly."

"What's that supposed to mean?" Trevor demanded. He paced restlessly in the confining room before looking pointedly at his watch. Through the window, he could see gray storm clouds gathering, their somber reflection darkening the clear waters of the Willamette River. Raindrops fell against the window, blurring his view.

Everett shifted uncomfortably in his chair and pushed his stocky fingers through his thinning hair. "Ever since the accident you've been obsessed with Stephens Timber."

"It began before the accident."

"Okay, ever since those phony charges last August, then."

Trevor turned to face the short man seated near a small table. "The charge was bribery," Trevor stated, his lips thinning.

"I know. But the important thing is that it was dropped." Everett looked as exasperated as he felt. "Admit it, Trevor, that is what all this—" his upturned palm rotated to indicate the packed bag "—is all about, isn't it?"

"Part of it," Trevor allowed with a grimace. "The bribery was just the latest of Lazarus's tricks. You seem to have conveniently forgotten that Lazarus Stephens was involved with my father's disappearance."

"Ten years ago. Idle speculation. No proof. Look, Trevor, you can't become obsessed with that all over again." Trevor's cold blue eyes didn't waver. Everett pressed his point home. "You can't fight a corporation the size of Stephens Timber, for God's sake! It employs over three thousand people in Oregon alone and Claud Stephens knows just whose palm he has to grease to get what he wants."

"But Claud only works for the company. He doesn't own it, does he?"

Everett changed his tactics when he noticed the dangerous glitter in Trevor's eyes. If there was anything Trevor Daniels enjoyed, it was a challenge.

"Look, Daniels, you've come too far too fast to throw it all away now. Forget what happened in the past, forget the accident, and the bribery scandal last summer, and, for God's sake, leave Stephens Timber alone!" Everett's expression was pleading. "Concentrate on the election in November."

"It's not that easy," Trevor admitted, rubbing his hand over the irritating pain in his abdomen.

"Rise above it."

Trevor's muscles flexed. "That's a little too much to ask, don't you think?"

Everett rolled his eyes upward and let out a frustrated sigh. "What I think is that you should quit brooding about false bribery charges and the accident," Everett explained with a lift of his shoulders. "Besides which, we have to make up for lost time. The days you spent in the hospital are gone; you missed a couple of very important meetings."

"They can be rescheduled," Trevor thought aloud. "Right now I have other things on my mind."

"You should be concentrating on the opposition."

"I am."

"Stephens Timber," Everett guessed, shaking his balding head despondently. "You're going to have to ease up on them."

"And play into Claud's greedy hands? No way."

"If you want to win the election—"

Trevor stopped dead in his tracks and wheeled around to confront his friend. Anger flared in his eyes. "I'm not even sure about that anymore. I had a lot of time to think while I was lying in that hospital. I'm not really sure that being a United States senator is all that it's cracked up to be. It certainly can't be worth the price."

"You're tired—"

"You bet I am!"

Everett held up his soft palms as if to ward off a blow, hoping that the gesture would calm Trevor. It didn't. Trevor had good reason to be upset, but Everett had hoped that the politician in Trevor Daniels would overcome the anger. "You've got to think about your career, Trevor, and you can't afford to take any time off right now. Think of all the hard work you've put into this campaign before you go mouthing off to the press about all of this nonsense concerning the accident. The last thing we need right now is another scandal!"

"Is that all you ever think about?"

"It's what you pay me to think about," Everett reminded his employer before draining the remainder of his warm drink. "My only concern is to get you into that vacant senatorial seat this fall."

"Even if it kills me?" Trevor asked with a sarcastic frown.

"Don't be ridiculous—"

"Then don't ridicule me!"

Everett's light eyes were steady when they clashed with Trevor's angry blue gaze. "I'm the guy who takes care of your security, remember? If I thought, I mean really thought that someone was out to get you, then I'd be the first one to suggest that you pull out of the race. But face it, if someone wanted to nail you, they would have done it before now. And, believe me, it wouldn't be some two-bit job on your car. Even the police didn't buy that one. For Christ's sake, don't turn paranoid on me now!" Everett muttered.

The words sunk into Trevor's weary mind. He let out his breath and his broad shoulders sagged. "Maybe you're right," he conceded, though his voice still sounded skeptical.

"Of course I am."

A crooked smile tugged at the hard corners of Trevor's rigid mouth. "I can think of a few times when you've been wrong."

"All in the past," Everett assured him with a knowing grin. "I don't claim to be infallible...just the nearest thing to it." The rotund campaign manager walked across the room and poured three stiff fingers of bourbon from a bottle sitting on the bar in the corner of the room. "Here, have a drink," he offered. "We both could use one."

After Trevor took the glass and swallowed some of the bourbon, Everett continued with his never-ending advice. "Now, whatever you do, try to forget about the accident and the scandal. Avoid the press at all costs until some of the noise dies down.

"Don't go spouting off about your car being sabotaged or you'll end up on the front page of the *Morning Surveyor* all over again. The last time was bad enough. Publicity from that rag, we don't need." Everett took a calming sip of liquor. He was somewhat satisfied that he had finally gotten through to Trevor, though it had taken a hell of a lot of talking. Trevor Daniels had a good chance of winning the primary in May, not to mention the election in November, if he didn't blow it by letting his hot temper control him. It was Everett's job to protect and mollify the would-be senator. That task might prove difficult if Trevor was hell-bent on seeing Ashley Stephens again.

Trevor set his empty glass on the bureau. He had tossed the campaign manager's words over in his mind, but despite Everett's warnings, the gleam of determination re-surfaced in Trevor's hard gaze. Trevor wasn't the kind of man to take things lying down, and never had been. His roguish charm and country-boy smile had won him many votes in the past, but it was his fierce determination that had brought him to the forefront of the political race for senator. Everett Woodward knew it as well as anyone. No amount of logic or smooth talk from Everett would change Trevor's mind once it was set.

"I want you to cancel all of my appointments for the next couple of days," Trevor said.

Everett sighed audibly. "Why?"

"I'm taking a little time off."

"Now?" Everett rose from the chair and eyed his employer suspiciously. "But you can't, Trevor. Not now. It's just not possible."

"Anything's possible. You're the one who gave me that advice when I first considered running."

"Exactly why you can't take a vacation now. Your schedule's a mess as it is. All that time you were recuper-ating—"

"From the accident," Trevor interjected. Everett opened his mouth to argue, but thought better of it. He knew just how far to push Trevor Daniels, and when to stop. "Think of my leave of absence as following doctor's orders for rest, if it will make you feel better," Trevor suggested.

"Is that what you want me to tell the press?"

The skin tightened over Trevor's cheekbones. "I don't give a damn what you tell them. Say whatever you want."

"You're not being very reasonable about this," Everett cautioned.

"That's because I don't feel very reasonable at the moment." Trevor hoisted the canvas bag off the bed and slung his jacket over his shoulder before turning toward the door.

"So, where are you going?"

"Away...alone."

"Alone?" Trevor's remark sounded dangerous to Everett and very much like the lie it was. Everett hesitated only slightly before playing his trump card. "I just hope you use your head, Daniels. And I hope that you're not going out on some personal vendetta against Stephens Timber Corporation. That wouldn't be wise—politically or personally."

Trevor's hand paused over the doorknob. He turned to face his concerned friend. "What's that supposed to mean?"

"It means that Ashley Stephens can't help you now," Everett said kindly. He noticed the stiffening of Trevor's spine and the sudden chilling of his gaze.

"Her name isn't Stephens anymore," Trevor stated. The tanned skin strained over Trevor's rugged features.

"But you and I both know that she and Richard Jennings were divorced several years ago. We also know that she owns the majority interest in Stephens Timber. Claud could be replaced in a minute, if Ashley decided to let him go."

The curse on Trevor's tongue was restrained. "You've done your homework," he observed, his voice cold.

Everett rubbed the tension from the back of his neck. "You pay me for that, too. Look, Trevor, I don't want to step out of line. What you do with your personal life is your business. I'm only worried when it begins to affect your career."

"So what are you suggesting?"

Genuine concern registered in the younger man's gaze. "Just be careful. Don't do anything, or get involved with anyone if you think there's a chance you might regret it later."

Trevor's voice was calm. "I'm not about to forget what's important in my life, if that's what you mean."

"The right woman sometimes can change a man's way of thinking."

Trevor frowned and turned the doorknob. "Then we really don't have much of a problem, do we? I think that you and I both agree that Ashley Jennings is definitely not 'the right woman.'"

With his final angry statement, Trevor jerked open the door and left his campaign manager to contemplate the half-empty bottle of bourbon.

Chapter Three

Ashley squinted into the darkness, watching warily as the snow piled around the edges of her windshield wipers. The mountain storm had come without warning and caught her off guard.

She had come to her father's Cascade Mountain retreat seeking solace. More than anything right now, she needed time alone to think things out. Now that her teaching obligations at the college had been fulfilled, she would be able to devote all of her energy to the timber company.

For the past week she had been in Portland, trying to sort through the books of Stephens Timber Corporation. As each day had passed it had become increasingly clear that Ashley couldn't trust her cousin Claud as far as she could throw him. There was little doubt in her mind that she would have to give him his walking papers as soon as she returned to Portland.

Armed with her briefcase full of financial reports concerning the operation of the vast timber empire, Ashley had spent the last two nights at the cabin poring over the accountant's figures concerning profit and loss, assets and liabilities and projected timber sales for the next two years.

Earlier in the afternoon she had pushed the neat computer printouts aside and decided to make a quick trip into Bend to replenish her dwindling grocery supply. On the way back to the cabin, the wind had picked up and within minutes powdery snow was falling from the heavens in a near-blizzard. The main highway was still clear, but the side roads, which already had an accumulation of snow, were quickly becoming impassable.

Her fingers tightened around the steering wheel and her thoughts wandered precariously to Trevor. In the short time since his accident, it seemed that there was no escaping him.

His engaging, slightly off-center smile had been photographed repeatedly and his rugged face had become incredibly newsworthy. Even last summer's scandal concerning alleged bribery charges hadn't tarnished his reputation; he was still considered by the local papers to have a lead in the primary election. Right now, Trevor Daniels was Oregon's favorite son, or soon would be, if the latest polls proved accurate.

According to Claud, Trevor's senatorial bid was sure to be a disaster for the company. Ashley disagreed. Trevor Daniels was too shrewd a politician to let personal rivalry interfere with his campaign. Besides which, Ashley was convinced that she couldn't trust Claud or his motives. What she had once considered a slight grudge against her because of Lazarus's will, Ashley now realized was a very deep flaw in Claud's character. For a fleeting moment she wondered if Trevor's accusations, which she had previously considered unlikely and vindictive, might be true.

Shifting gears as the Jeep started to climb the rugged terrain, Ashley thought about the events leading up to Trevor's sudden prominence and fame. Senator Higgins's fatal heart attack had left a vacant seat in Washington, D.C., and public opinion seemed to think that Trevor would be elected to fill the void.

Well, at least he got what he wanted, Ashley chided herself, feeling a trace of the old bitterness return. *That's a lot more than you can say for yourself.*

The tires slid on the snow-packed mountain road before holding the vehicle steady on the slippery gravel. "Just a little farther," Ashley coaxed.

Slowly she turned the steering wheel toward the narrow lane angling up the steep hillside. She frowned as she noticed ruts in the newly fallen snow. There were only two other pieces of property bordering hers and the mountain retreats that occupied those adjacent parcels were used for summer homes. Or at least they had been.

But this was her first visit to the cabin in several years. Perhaps the neighboring houses were being used over the Christmas holidays. She found the thought that she wasn't completely alone in the remote section of the mountains comforting. Though she had come seeking solitude, she now appreciated the knowledge that there was someone nearby in case the storm became more violent.

Once again Ashley's thoughts turned to Trevor and his recent accident. Though it had occurred only a week ago, she still couldn't forget about it and found herself wondering how he was doing. Her telephone calls to the hospital had never been returned and when she had tried to see him again, she had been thwarted by a determined security guard. Ashley got the message: Trevor didn't want to see her.

She couldn't blame him. For all practical purposes, she owned Stephens Timber Corporation, a corporation that in the past had represented everything in the timber industry Trevor opposed. Though she was forcing changes within the company it would still be a long time before some of the old techniques could be abandoned for safer, more environmentally sound modes of timber harvest.

"You're a fool," she admonished, and caught her lower lip with her teeth. She tried to concentrate while crossing the remaining distance to the cabin, but couldn't help hoping that Trevor had recovered from the injuries he'd sustained in the accident. How had the accident affected his career—*his damned career?* Were his eyes still as incredibly blue and erotic as they once had been?

"Damn it, Ashley," she swore, her knuckles whitening over the steering wheel, "why can't you forget that man? He never loved you—he just used you...."

The pain in his side hadn't subsided. With each passing minute it throbbed more sharply, growing until a dull headache pounded mercilessly behind his eyes. Trevor had overexerted himself and he was paying dearly for it.

The long drive had fatigued him and set his nerves on edge. Just the thought of seeing Ashley again disturbed him more than he would like to admit.

After fumbling in the pocket of his jeans he extracted a small vial of pills. He was chilled to the bone and the raw ache under his shirt throbbed mercilessly. Disgusted with himself and seeing the prescribed medication as a sign of weakness, he dropped the small brown bottle on the table and ignored it.

"Damn it!" Trevor cursed to himself as he reached for his neglected glass of Scotch. The liquor was warm and did little to relieve the dull ache in his abdomen.

Though his muscles were cramped from the cold, he could feel the warm trickle of sweat running down the back of his neck. He absently rubbed his forehead and wondered how much longer he would have to wait for Ashley to return. Leaning back in the chair, he closed his eyes and listened to the sounds of the night. Presently, the liquor started to take effect. The ache in his head was beginning to subside and the razor-sharp edge of his mind dulled slightly, sacrificed for the freedom from pain. He sat rigidly in the leather chair, his wet jeans clinging stiffly to his legs, while he sipped the remains of his distasteful drink.

The rumble of an approaching vehicle's engine caught his attention. Headlights flashed against the far wall, illuminating the rustic room. It was a place Trevor remembered well, a room where he had spent many lazy afternoons in years past. It was the very spot where he had first felt Ashley's trembling surrender. It had been early spring. They had run into the cabin to escape the sudden shower. He could still smell the fresh, damp scent of her black hair, taste the raindrops that had run down her cheeks. It seemed like a lifetime ago. How long had it been? Seven years? Eight? His mind was too cloudy to recall and it really didn't matter. He didn't give a damn about Ashley...at least not anymore.

The engine was killed and a car door slammed. Trevor had to force himself to remain patient. All of his senses were alert, his raw nerves stretched paper-thin. It had taken the better part of three days to track Ashley down and when he had finally found her, he had been pleased in a perverse sort of way. He found it ironic that Ashley had chosen to return to the cabin. It seemed to justify his reason for being here.

The key turned in the lock. Trevor heard the sound of cold metal resisting intrusion. Though he sat in another room, he could clearly see the entrance of the cabin from his vantage point in the darkness.

As the door was pushed open, Trevor narrowed his eyes. It was too dark to see clearly, but Trevor quickly determined that the small form brushing snow off her jacket and stamping her boots on the hall carpet was Ashley. As he watched her voyeuristically, the sour taste of deception rose in his throat.

He had hoped that he would feel loathing when he saw her again, but the contempt he had cultivated had refused to grow. His fingers tensed around the arm of the chair when her gaze swept past the door of the den. She pulled off her stocking cap and let her long, dark hair tumble free. Trevor's lips compressed into an unforgiving line of disgust; she was more beautiful than he had remembered.

Ashley hesitated a moment, thinking that the cabin felt different somehow, and then with a frown shrugged off the disturbing feeling and set the bag of groceries on an antique sideboard while she removed her boots and jacket. After hanging the ski jacket on the curved arm of the hall tree, she picked up the groceries, walked into the kitchen and put on a pot of tea as she replenished her cupboards.

The teapot had just begun to whistle when an unexpected noise made her heart miss a beat. "Ashley." The sound of her name made her gasp. It came from a male voice that was darkly familiar. She rotated quickly to confront the intruder.

The man was standing in the doorway to the den. "Oh my God," Ashley whispered, barely believing the apparition. Her eyes were captured in the shadowy depths of his blue gaze.

"Ashley," he repeated slowly, as if he knew how much of a shock he had imposed upon her. His voice caught on her name and it carried her backward to a past in which she had shared her life, her love with him. "I didn't mean to frighten you," he said softly.

Her throat was suddenly desert-dry, and she felt the sting of wistful tears burn against her eyelids. Her step forward was hesitant, as if she expected him to vanish as quickly as he had appeared. "What are you doing here? How did you get in?" Her voice was a muted whisper and her sea-green eyes were filled with a thousand questions spanning eight years.

"I hope I didn't startle you," he stated. "I...wanted to make sure that you were alone."

Though her smile was fragile, her round eyes never wavered. "Why are you here, Trevor?" she asked, finding her voice. "Why now?" All of Claud's warnings caused a painful wrenching of her heart.

The small light of defiance in her gaze bothered him. He felt the need to apologize but ignored it. He had planned this night for nearly two weeks and had never once considered that he might feel compelled to explain himself to her. His lips thinned as he reminded himself that she was the one who had to account for what was happening to him. His blue eyes held her transfixed.

"I got your message at the hospital."

"But you didn't call."

"I wanted to see you in person—"

"I came by the hospital."

"—alone."

Ashley's heart missed a beat but she forced herself to appear calm. She couldn't—wouldn't—let Trevor use her again. If he was here, it was for a reason, and she couldn't delude herself into thinking that it was just to be with her once more.

Trevor frowned at his own admission. "I thought it would be better for everyone concerned if we talked in private." He seemed sincere. But then, he had once before. She felt the old bitterness return.

"Are you sure that would be wise, Senator? What if your constituents found out that you were talking to the owner of Stephens Timber Corporation? Wouldn't that ruin your credibility?"

For a breathless instant anger sparked in his eyes. "We can start this by going for each other's throats, Ashley, but I don't think that would accomplish much, do you?"

"I suppose not." She walked past him and flipped the switch on a brass table lamp. The room was instantly illuminated in a bath of dim light. Ashley's smile trembled as she looked at him. Trevor appeared to have aged five years in the past month. Yet he was still the most intriguing man she had ever met. His cold blue eyes were just as enigmatic as she remembered.

It took a few moments for the shock of seeing him again to wear off. "I'm having a little trouble understanding why you're here," she stated, still trying to hold on to her shattered poise. It was obvious that he had been sitting in the leather chair near the fire. Ashley took a seat on the edge of an overstuffed couch and tucked one foot beneath her. The fabric of her jeans stretched over her leg

muscles, and Trevor was forced to shift his gaze back to
the concerned expression on her elegant face.

It was still unlined, a perfect oval of alabaster skin with
large, even features, lofty cheekbones and a sparkle of
innocence that danced in her eyes when she laughed. Tonight her eyes were sober and suspicious. Her skin was
flushed slightly from the cold, and her dark, finely
arched brows drew downward in concentration as she
tried to understand the man who was silently regarding
her.

"Okay, Trevor, I'm sitting down and I think I'm about
as calm as I'm going to get," she said.

"Good." His gaze was stony and cold.

Ashley had always had a powerful effect on him in the
past and time hadn't made Trevor immune to the seductive curve of her chin or the trace of sadness in her wistful smile. Trevor had to force himself to remember the
reason for coming to the lonely cabin in the remote
stretch of mountains. It would be damnably easy to forget the rest of the world tonight. All too easily Ashley
could entrance him and he would fall victim to the subtle allure of her slow smile.

Ashley shook her dark curls, as if to clear her mind.
Dear God, what was Trevor doing here? "This is quite a
shock, you know. I thought that..."

"You thought that I was recuperating from an
accident."

"Yes."

"I was," he admitted in a rough whisper. Though he
sat away from the light, Ashley could see his sharply de-

fined features. His strong face no longer held the warmth she remembered, and deep lines of worry webbed from the corners of his eyes.

"And now that you feel up to it, you decided to break into my cabin. Right? That's against the law, Senator."

"I've been charged with worse." There was a viciousness in his words that she didn't understand until she remembered the bribery charges. She studied his face. His chin was still bold and square, but his cheeks had hollowed, probably because of the accident. A tiny scar, still an angry red line, cut across his jaw. Beneath his eyes were dark shadows, evidence of too many sleepless nights. When he stared at her she saw no trace of emotion on the rugged contours of his face, but she read something in the chill of his gaze. He looked haunted. "Trevor...what's going on?"

"I want to know just how desperate Stephens Timber is to get me out of the senatorial race."

"*I* have nothing against your politics, you know that."

A disdainful black brow cocked. "What I know is that for all practical purposes, you own Stephens Timber, right?"

The brutal glare in his eyes forced the truth from her lips. "Except for a few shares—"

"But your cousin, Claud, he's the general manager— the guy who's responsible for the day-to-day operations?"

"Claud reports to me. Look, Trevor, I don't know what you're getting at, and I really don't see that I'm obligated to tell you anything. Just what the devil is going on?'' Her mysterious green eyes pleaded with him.

Light from the antique lamp diffused into the far corners of the room, making the shadows dangerously intimate. Scarlet embers smoldered in the fire, just as they did on the first night she and Trevor had made love. Time might have hurried past them, but Ashley knew she would never love another man with the reckless, unbound passion she had felt for Trevor.

Trevor's eyes darkened, as if his thoughts had taken the same precarious path as hers. Passion flickered in their midnight depths before he jerked his gaze away from her to study the fire. It was as if, in that one hesitant moment, he had inadvertently divulged too much of himself to her.

Ashley reached over and brushed the back of his hand with hers. With a jolt, his head snapped backward and his eyes drove into hers. Gone was any trace of desire. In its stead lurked cruel suspicion, lingering just below the surface of his gaze, silently accusing her of a crime she couldn't begin to comprehend.

She withdrew her hand. Her fingers trembled as she pushed her hair out of her eyes. Dread crawled up her spine. ''This has something to do with your accident, doesn't it?''

''I'm not sure it was an accident.''

Ashley was stunned. Perhaps she hadn't heard him correctly. ''But the papers said—''

''I know what they said. I know what the police report said. But I'm not convinced.''

"Wait a minute." She closed her eyes in order to clear her mind. There had been too many emotional shocks tonight and her tangled feelings were interfering with her logic. Stretching her fingers outward in a supplicating gesture, she begged for his patience. The rumors of foul play entered her mind and she shuddered. "Let's start over...."

His frown became a poignant smile. "A little late for that, wouldn't you say?" The sarcasm in his words sliced into her heart.

She bit back the hot retort forming on her tongue. She folded her hands over one knee and forced herself to remain as calm as possible. "I think it's about time you leveled with me. You owe me that much."

"I owe you nothing."

Her frayed nerves got the better of her and her thin patience snapped. "That's where you're wrong, Trevor," she contradicted. "First, you broke into my place after trudging God only knows how long in the snow—just to hide your truck. Next, you sat in the dark in order to scare the living daylights out of me, which, by the way, you did. Then, you end up making vague accusations and ridiculous insinuations that don't mean a damned thing to me! I keep getting the impression that you're waiting for me to say something...or fall into some kind of trap, but I can't for the life of me figure out what it is! What happened to you, Trevor? Just what the hell happened to you and what's all this nonsense about your accident—"

"I've told you before, I don't think it was an accident."

She lifted her arm as if to ward off another verbal assault. "Yeah, I know," she mumbled while placing her hand on the arm of the chair and pushing herself out of it. She stretched before bending over and examining the contents of the basket of wood sitting near the fireplace. She needed an excuse for time to gather her scattered thoughts.

Tossing a large piece of oak onto the coals, Ashley slid a secretive glance in Trevor's direction. The crackle of flames shattered the silence as the fire began to consume the new log. Returning her gaze to her task, Ashley spread her palms open to the warmth of the flames and didn't bother to turn her head or look at Trevor when she spoke. With practiced calm she asked, "I've known you for a long time, haven't I?"

"Eight years," he supplied, eyeing her backside as she kneeled before the ravenous flames. He couldn't help but consider her supple curves. Her jeans were stretched tightly over her buttocks, leaving little room for his imagination. For a fleeting moment he wondered if her skin was still as soft as it once had been.

"Eight years, that's right," she agreed. "In those eight years I've called you a lot of things." His dark brows raised inquisitively when she paused. "But I've never accused you of being a lunatic." She dusted her hands on her jeans and smiled to herself as she stood. She was content to run her fingers over the rough wood of the oak mantel as she continued. "So you see, you're going to have a difficult time convincing me that you drove over a thirty-foot embankment intentionally.''

"Of course not.''

The first cold feelings of doubt had already taken hold of her. What was it Claud had said? That Trevor was still convinced that Stephens Timber had something to do with his father's disappearance?

He studied her quietly, watching the gentle curve of her neck as she laid her head against the mantel. Her ebony hair brushed against her white skin when she pushed it over her shoulder. Her round eyes were filled with concern and worry for him.

When Trevor rose from the chair too quickly, a dizzying sensation swept over him in a sickening wave. The pain in his side was once again beginning to throb. Grimacing against the dull ache, he made his way over to the fireplace and propped his shoulder against the warm stones. He pressed his hand against his abdomen until the ache subsided.

Holding her transfixed with his sober gaze, he spoke. When he did, the skin tightened over the rugged planes of his face and his eyes glinted with renewed determination. "Look, Ashley. I didn't intend to lose control of the car, you know that as well as I do.''

Ashley's heart was thudding with dread. In her anxiety, she ran her fingers through the thick strands of her blue-black hair. Letting her forehead drop to her palm, she gently massaged her temple. Her voice was ragged, barely a whisper. "Then what you're suggesting is that someone tried to kill you.''

"Not just someone, Ashley." His eyes drove into hers. "I think Claud hired someone to tamper with my car." Trevor's hand reached out and took hold of her wrist.

Ashley's breath caught in her throat. "That's preposterous!"

"I don't think so," he retorted. She tried to pull away from him, but he wouldn't release her arm. Dark blue eyes, the color of midnight, impaled her. "I think you'd better tell me everything you know about your cousin."

"This is insane," she managed to say, though her throat was constricting her breath. "I'm the first one to admit that Claud isn't a saint, but you can't go around accusing him of trying to kill you, for God's sake."

"Not until I have proof."

"Which you don't?"

"Not yet."

"Then how can you even suggest that he's involved?"

"Gut feeling."

"That won't hold up in court, Senator. But you know that, don't you? Or at least you should since you're a lawyer."

"Ashley, look, I know that I'm right."

She read the determination in his angry blue gaze. "And you want me to help you prove that Claud was trying to kill you, right? Trevor, you've got to be joking."

"I'm dead serious. I know that Claud and your father paid that mill owner in Molalla to file those bribery charges!"

"How?" Her green eyes sparked with indignant fury. "How do you know that? Did the man tell you?" Her lips turned downward in repressed rage and she pulled her hand free of his grasp.

"The police were convinced that the charges were false. They dropped the case."

"But what proof do you have that my father was behind it?"

"That mill, which had been on the verge of bankruptcy, was suddenly operational again."

"Circumstantial evidence, counselor." She waved her hand frantically in the air. "And even if your suspicions are right, who are you to say that my father was behind it?"

"I checked. Who do you think supplies that mill with rough timber?"

"I couldn't hazard a guess," she lied, knowing what he was insinuating. Her heart was like a trip-hammer in her rib cage.

"Then you're not doing your job, Ashley. The primary customer for Watkins Mill in Molalla is Stephens Timber." Trevor began to pace the floor in long, agitated strides.

"I don't understand you, Trevor," Ashley said, her voice beginning to tremble. "My father and Claud both warned me that you had some sort of personal vendetta against the timber company but I never believed them—"

"Until now?"

She nodded her head. Hot tears of frustration burned in her eyes as she stared at the only man whom she had ever loved. "Is it because of me?"

His pacing halted. He stood with his back to her and she could see the muscles of his shoulders tensing beneath the soft cotton fabric of his shirt. "No, Ashley, this started long before I knew you—"

"Because of your father's disappearance."

He turned on his heel and when he looked at her his eyes were filled with the torture he had suffered for nearly ten years. He didn't need to answer.

"Then Claud was right. You have a grudge." She closed her eyes against the truth. "You really don't think much of me, do you?"

"It's your family I wonder about."

"To the point that you would go out of your way to prove them guilty of anything." She shook her head in confusion and light from the fire caught in the ebony strands of her hair. "I own the company now. You know that I wouldn't be involved in anything illegal—"

"And I also know that you weren't in control of the corporation when my father disappeared, or when those phony charges were filed, or when my car was sabotaged."

"If it was."

"I have a mechanic who will back me up."

She ran her fingers nervously through her hair, but her eyes never left his. "Why did you come here, Trevor? What is it exactly that you expect of me?"

His blue eyes never left her face and he pinched his lower lip between his thumb and forefinger pensively. "I want you to go through all of the company records and look for anything that might prove my theories."

"Wait a minute—you want my help in proving that Stephens Timber and my family were involved in something illegal?" She was incredulous.

His voice was low and steady. It sent a shiver as cold as the black night down her spine. "What I want from you, Ashley, is the truth."

Ashley's mouth was suddenly desert-dry. Her voice was barely a whisper. "And when I go through all the company records and I find nothing, what then?"

"All I want is the truth."

She weighed the alternatives in her mind as she reached her decision. "Okay, Trevor, I'll look through everything. But I want something in return."

"I wouldn't expect anything else from Lazarus Stephens's daughter."

"When I check all the records and clear my father's name, I expect you to make a public statement." His dark brows rose inquisitively. "A statement that ends once and for all the bitterness between our two families and a statement that absolves my father of all the charges you've attributed to him."

Trevor considered her request. "How do I know that you'll be honest with me?"

Her chin inched upward defiantly. "I guess you'll just have to trust me," she murmured. "I realize that might be difficult for you, but I don't see that you have much of a choice."

His eyes darkened. "I'll need proof, Ashley. I'll give you my public announcement, if you can prove to me that your family hasn't been involved in the accident, the bribery or my father's disappearance."

Her confidence wavered. "I'll let you know."

Trevor reached for his coat and Ashley's heart dropped. He had reappeared so suddenly in her life; she couldn't let go of him—not yet. There were so many memories they had shared, so much time that had separated them. Desperately she clung to the thread of hope that he still cared for her. "You can't leave," she whispered, her heart in her throat. He paused, one arm thrust into the suede jacket.

"Why not?"

"The storm—it's nearly a blizzard."

His eyes darkened ominously. "What are you suggesting, Ms Jennings? That I spend the night, here, alone with you?"

Chapter Four

Eight years seemed to roll backward as she stared into Trevor's smoldering blue eyes. His gaze touched the most feminine part of her soul and made her voice husky.

"You can't leave in this storm," Ashley repeated. "You'll have to wait until it dies down."

His eyes darted to the frosted windowpanes before returning to search her worried face. "That might not be until morning." Trevor slowly advanced upon her, his eyes lingering thoughtfully on the concerned knit of her brow. His voice was dangerously low. "Do you really think it would be wise for me to stay?" he asked as he reached her. Slowly, his fingers traced the elegant curve of her jaw.

He noticed the hesitation in her sensual sea-green eyes. "I don't think you have much of a choice."

Trevor's hands stopped their loving exploration and his gaze hardened. "That's where you're wrong, Ms Jennings." He shoved his arms into the sleeves of his jacket and flashed a smile as bitterly cold as the night. "All I need from you is a lift to the Lamberts'."

Her brows quirked. "You're staying at the Lambert place?"

"That's right."

She stepped away from him and eyed him suspiciously. "Just how long have you been planning this?" she asked, tilting her palm upward and making a sweeping gesture to include everything that had transpired within the walls of the intimate room.

"Since my car went out of control and rolled down a thirty-foot embankment."

Her spine stiffened slightly. "You really believe that Claud was behind the accident, don't you?"

"If I didn't, I wouldn't be here." Eyes as cold as glass pierced hers. His voice was devoid of emotion and Ashley realized with a welling sense of disappointment how little he cared for her.

She shook her head and sighed. "I can't believe that anyone, not even Claud, would want you dead."

"I don't think he wanted to kill me, just shake me up a little. Scare me. And that, dear lady, he accomplished."

"But why?" Before he could answer she held up her hand and chewed on her lower lip. "Because of the election. You think that he's so paranoid you might win, that he set up the accident to warn you in hope that you might back out, right?''

"That's the way I have it figured."

Ashley managed a humorless smile. "I think you've been reading too many spy stories lately, Senator. Your entire theory reads like some cheap James Bond rip-off."

"Maybe that's because you can't see the truth when it stares you in the face, Ashley," he suggested with a frown. Deep furrows lined his forehead and surrounded the tense corners of his mouth. "But then you never have been able to sort fact from fiction where your family is concerned. You probably still don't believe that Stephens Timber was responsible for the ecological disaster near Springfield."

"My father denied it," Ashley whispered.

"But you know better, don't you? Your father's company was spraying with a dangerous pesticide, Ashley. Probably because Lazarus recommended it. It was effective and cheap."

"No one knew it was dangerous—"

Trevor's eyes glittered ominously. "There had already been cases linking that pesticide with health hazards. The FDA was in the process of banning it. But your father didn't listen and the people living near the area that was being sprayed paid for it, didn't they?"

"It was never proven—"

"That's a cop-out, Ashley and you know it. Maybe you just preferred to hide your head in the sand. You didn't have to look into the eyes of the people when they found out that they were dying. The effects of the spray sometimes take months to show up, but when they do, the result is the same—a slow and painful death.''

"No one knows if the pesticide was the cause."

"Yet. Researchers are still working on it." The skin stretched tightly over Trevor's harsh features as he remembered the day he had to revise Dennis Lange's will. Dennis was only thirty-three when he had come to Trevor's office, and mentioned that he had some of the symptoms of the pesticide poisoning. Dennis had died six months later, leaving a young widow and three-year-old daughter. Trevor had vowed on his friend's grave that if he ever was in a position of power, he would fight against the indiscriminate use of chemicals on the environment. "Your father knew about the hazards, it was just more convenient to ignore them."

Masking the fact that his words had wounded her heart, Ashley turned, walked out of the room, grabbed her jacket and reached into a downy pocket for the keys to the Jeep. She had already pulled on her boots, zipped the ski jacket to her neck and wound her hair into her stocking cap by the time Trevor joined her in the small foyer. "Let's go," she whispered while purposely avoiding the silent questions in his bold eyes.

The Lambert cabin was only a little over a mile up the hill, but the drive took nearly ten minutes because of the snow that had drifted over the seldom-used road. The storm wasn't nearly as fierce as it had been, but large flakes still drifted leisurely to the ground and danced in the bright beams of the headlights.

Though it was nearly nine o'clock, it seemed like daylight. The pristine drifts of snow, settled carelessly against the trunks of graceful Ponderosa pines, gave the night a blue-gray illumination. Clumps of pine needles protruded proudly from their winter cloak of white and the shadowy mountains blended into the dark sky.

Ashley had to wipe the windshield with a cloth as condensation collected on the cold glass. The Jeep hit a patch of ice. One tire spun wildly, causing the vehicle to slide on the slippery terrain and roughly tossing the passengers against the dash. Trevor winced in pain when his shoulder was thrust against the door.

"Are you all right?" Ashley asked, when the wheels of the Jeep were securely gripping the gravel once again. Her elegant face was pinched with concern.

"Just great," Trevor replied sarcastically. "Thanks to your cousin Claud."

Ashley pursed her lips together angrily and the remainder of the trip was made in mutual silence.

Lights were glowing in the paned windows of the Lambert cabin. Trevor's pickup was parked near the garage. Nearly three inches of snow had piled on the hood and roof of the truck.

Ashley stopped the Jeep and pulled on the emergency brake, but let the engine idle. She turned to face Trevor and found that he was staring thoughtfully at her. His eyes were deep blue and sensual. They seemed to caress her face.

"You could come in," he invited, tugging gently on her stocking cap and allowing her hair to fall in wisping black curls around her face. Her breath caught in her throat at the intimacy of the gesture.

"I...I don't think so," she whispered, shaking her head and avoiding his probing stare. "It would be best, for both of us, if I left."

When his fingers softly touched her temple, they trembled. Ashley closed her eyes and moved her head away from his persuasive touch. "You'll be okay, won't you...by yourself?" she asked, thinking of his injury. In the close quarters of the Jeep, it was difficult not to feel the urgency of his touch.

"I'll manage," he said, his voice tight.

"You're sure?"

"I'm used to doing things on my own, Ashley," he reminded her. "I can take care of myself."

"And that's why you spent a week in the hospital."

His jaw clenched furiously as he reached for the handle of the door. "You can blame Claud for that one."

Ashley's hand, which had still clung to the steering wheel, reached out to clutch his arm. "Let's not argue," she implored. "It's time to stop this fighting before it gets to the point where it can't be stopped."

For a breathless instant, there was silence. Snowflakes gathered on the windshield, providing a protective curtain from the rest of the world. His eyes searched the innocent wisdom in her gaze.

"Why did I ever let you go?" he asked himself, his blue eyes filled with dark self-mockery.

She swallowed against the dryness in her throat as, slowly, he lowered his head and his lips brushed tenderly against hers. How long had she waited for this moment? She sighed and one hand slid beneath his jacket to touch him gently on the neck. Old emotions, long dormant, began to assail the most intimate parts of her. His kiss was flavored with the hint of Scotch and reminded her of a time, somewhere in the distant past of her carefree youth, when they had made love in a fragrant field of clover.

"I've missed you," he whispered as he reluctantly pulled his lips from hers. "Dear God, Ashley, I've missed you." His strong arms held her close to him and he buried his face in the thick ebony strands of her hair. "Stay with me."

A sob, filled with the raw ache of eight forgotten years, broke from her lips. The warmth and protection of his embrace was all she had ever wanted. She leaned her forehead against his neck and she closed her eyes against the feelings ripping her apart. She had vowed never to let this man touch her again and yet she couldn't let go.

She could hear the sound of his heartbeat, feel the warmth of his breath as it whispered in her hair. Her heart wrenched painfully as she remembered how brutally he had thrust her out of his life and she knew that she could never trust him again.

"I...I have to go," she stated, her voice quaking with the small lie. She couldn't allow her vulnerability for Trevor to overcome her common sense.

"Why?"

"I have things I've got to accomplish."

"Such as?"

"Such as start looking through the company books. At your request."

Gently he released her. His lips were pulled into a thoughtful line of disbelief. "That's just an excuse, Ashley. You're afraid of me, aren't you?"

She let out a ragged breath. "No, Trevor, I'm not afraid of you, as a man or as a senator. But I am afraid of what becoming involved with you might mean."

"I don't understand."

She avoided his gaze and stared out the partially covered windshield. "I've worked a long time to become an independent woman. All my life I've had some man telling me what to do. First Dad, then you and finally Richard."

At the mention of her ex-husband's name, Trevor's muscles tightened. "I don't want to get involved with a man for a while," she murmured. "Not until I'm certain that I can stand on my own two feet."

"Haven't you been doing that?"

She nodded. "For several years. But now I have to prove myself—to myself."

"With the timber company," he guessed. "The last thing I would have expected from you, Ashley, is that you would turn into a latent feminist." He raked frustrated fingers through his chestnut-colored hair. "I thought you liked living in the lap of luxury."

She turned her mysterious eyes back on him. "There are a lot of things you don't know about me," Ashley suggested, smiling wistfully. "Maybe someday we'll talk about them. But...right now, I need time, Trevor. Time to think about you and me, about what we meant to each other and about everything that has happened between your family and mine.''

He frowned, his dark brows blunted in vexation, but he seemed to accept what she said. ''This is your decision, Ashley,'' Trevor reminded her. Then, with more dexterity than she thought him capable of, he opened the door of the Jeep, climbed out of the vehicle and walked, head bent, toward the front door. As he opened the door to the rustic Lambert home, he turned toward her. Ashley imagined that he was inviting her inside. She swallowed against the ache in her throat at the sight of him standing in the snow.

Somehow Ashley managed a weak wave before she put the Jeep in reverse, released the brake and headed back to her cabin. The picture of Trevor standing on the small porch in the darkness, with snowflakes clinging to his wavy chestnut hair, stayed with her on the short trip home.

Once back in her own cabin, she brushed the snow off her shoulders, hung the jacket on the hall tree and hurried into the den. After checking her watch and contemplating the wisdom of her actions, she dialed the number of John Ellis, accountant for Stephens Timber Corporation.

The young accountant answered on the third ring. ''John, this is Ashley. I know it's late, but I need a favor.''

''Anything,'' was the congenial reply.

"Can you send me a copy of all transactions that have occurred at the company for the last eight months?"

There was a weighty pause on the other end of the line. "What do you mean by 'all the transactions'?"

"I mean everything—general ledger, checkbook, computer entries, expenses, payroll, the works."

"That's a lot of information...I suppose you want to audit the books of every branch—"

"I do. But let's start with Portland."

"You're joking," he said tonelessly while contemplating the magnitude of the task.

"No. Sorry, John, but I'm dead serious."

"Great. I figured as much." Ashley could almost hear the wheels turning in the young accountant's head. Despite his grumbling, John loved to scour the books. "And I suppose you want it tonight?"

"That would be nice, but I'll settle for tomorrow."

"Tomorrow!" John's anxious voice indicated that he thought she had just asked for the moon.

"Look, I realize that everything won't be available, but just start sending things to the Bend office through the computer. I'll pick up the first set of figures around three in the afternoon and then I'll get anything else on Thursday."

"You make it sound so easy—"

"I knew I could count on you. Thanks."

"Don't thank me yet. You might be asking the impossible."

"Don't I always?"

There was an amused chuckle on the other end of the line. "Yep. I suppose you do."

"Then you're going to love this. I'd like all the records for each branch available next week when I'm back in Portland."

"Is that all?" he asked sarcastically.

"Just one more thing. I want you to keep this confidential. Don't tell anyone at the office what I'm doing. Not even Claud."

There was silence on the other end for a moment. "You think someone's embezzling, don't you?" the accountant thought aloud.

"I hope not," Ashley murmured fervently. "God, I hope not." She replaced the receiver carefully and a small shiver of dread ran down her spine. What had she gotten herself into? If she found nothing in the books, Trevor still wouldn't be convinced that she was telling the truth. And, if she did discover that someone in the company was skimming money from the corporation to sabotage Trevor's campaign, she would only prove that all of the rumors that had circulated about Stephens Timber were true. Either way, it was a no-win situation.

Ashley opened her eyes against an intruding beam of sunlight, which was flooding the room in the soft silvery hues of winter. The sheets on the small bed were ice cold. Ashley hurriedly reached for her velour robe lying at the foot of the bed. As quickly as her cold fingers could accomplish the task, she pulled the soft blue garment over her shivering body.

Tying the belt under her breasts, she raced down the steps leading from the loft and quickly restarted the fire in the den. Then, intent on putting on a hot pot of coffee and rebuilding the fire in the wood stove, she hurried into the kitchen. She was rubbing her forearms briskly as she entered the kitchen but she stopped dead in her tracks when she viewed the littered kitchen table.

Strewn carelessly over the smooth maple surface were dozens of pieces of paper. Computer printouts, general correspondence and financial statements were piled on the table without any trace of organization.

Ashley pulled an exaggerated frown at the documents as she walked over to the stove and lit the fire. So much for Trevor's theory. Nothing in the documents even remotely hinted at foul play. She had been awake until nearly two in the morning poring over the documents she had brought with her from Portland. True, she had just barely scratched the surface of the company records, but she felt an incredible sense of relief that all the books for the last month seemed in perfect order. "Put that in your mouth and chew on it a while, Senator," she whispered vindictively to herself. Then, without warning, a distant memory of Trevor, which she had locked away in a dark corner of her mind, came vividly back to her. His thick brown hair was rumpled, his muscled torso naked and bronze against pale wintergreen sheets, and as he had reached for her, his sleepy blue eyes had sparked with rekindled passion....

Stop it, Ashley! she demanded. *It's over. When are you going to accept the fact that he never loved you?* But the thought of last night and his tender embrace nagged at her and contradicted her angry words. Last night, she had felt his need, witnessed his restraint and known that he still cared for her, if only just a little.

Forcing herself to ignore the traitorous yearnings which had begun to flow within her veins just at the thought of his kiss, Ashley went through the motions of brewing coffee. She couldn't afford to feel anything for Trevor—not now, not ever. The pain of the past had left her too vulnerable and scarred and she had vowed never to be trapped by his erotic eyes again.

When the kitchen began to warm up and the coffee was perking, Ashley straightened the corporate reports and put them into her briefcase before she went back to the loft, discarded her robe and headed for a hot shower. The warm water was invigorating as it splashed against her skin and hair. Softly, she began to hum.

By the time she had towel-dried and slipped into a clean pair of jeans and sweater, she could smell the inviting aroma of coffee wafting through the small cabin. Without bothering to put on her shoes, Ashley made her way down the stairs and padded over the scattered throw rugs and oak floors to the kitchen.

"Good morning," Trevor remarked as she raced through the open archway separating the den from the kitchen. Ashley's heart jumped to her throat.

She hesitated slightly at the shock of seeing him again. In the daylight he seemed more real than he had in the shadowy night. His eyes were as clear and blue as the mountain sky and the enigmatic smile that had trapped her in the past was neatly in place. Her heart hammered excitedly for a moment, but then reality returned to her. Indignant fire sizzled in her sea-green eyes. "Don't you know how to knock, for God's sake? Or do you just get a kick out of breaking in and scaring the living daylights out of me?"

His easy smile was self-assured and his blue eyes twinkled in amusement as he took a sip of his coffee.

"Help yourself," she mocked with a severe frown.

"Still have a sweet disposition in the morning, I see," he remarked before lifting his cup. "Join me?"

"Don't you have anything better to do than a bad impression of a cat burglar?"

He raised his hands in protest. "I haven't stolen anything—"

"Yet." She took a chair opposite him at the table and accepted the coffee he had already poured for her. It was laced with sugar and cream. Just the way she liked it. "I drink it black—"

"Since when?"

"Since I got a little older and have to watch my weight."

Again his blue eyes sparked with humor. He cocked his head in the direction of her cup. "Go ahead," he suggested, "indulge yourself. Sin a little."

Her dark brows raised fractionally but she managed a smile.

"By the way, I did knock," Trevor announced, "but no one answered."

"I must have been—"

"In the shower," Trevor finished for her. Ashley nodded and smiled into her cup. "When you didn't answer, I got worried. After I came into the cabin, I realized you were in the bathroom, but it didn't seem to make much sense to go back outside and wait in the cold while you took your sweet time upstairs. I think we know each other well enough not to worry about formalities."

She was forced to smile, but the familiar caress of his eyes encouraged her to shift her gaze out the window to stare at the soft accumulation of snow. "How did you get in?"

He reached into his pocket, withdrew a dull piece of metal, and tossed it onto the table.

Ashley's heart missed a beat as she turned her attention to the object and touched the cold metal. "The key—how?" she began to ask, but her voice caught and faded. She had given the key to Trevor eight years ago, during Indian summer when they had met in secret tryst at the cabin. Tears, unwanted and filled with silent agony, stung the backs of her eyelids. Silently she dropped the key back onto the table.

"I never threw it away," he said solemnly. There was a wistful sadness in his gaze.

"You kept it all these years?" Her voice had grown husky.

He nodded and frowned thoughtfully into the black depths of his coffee.

The telephone rang shrilly and disrupted the intimate atmosphere which had surrounded them. Ashley was glad for an excuse to leave the table and avoid the unasked questions in Trevor's bold eyes.

"Hello?" she called into the receiver as she brushed the hot tears aside.

"Ashley. It's John."

Ashley managed a smile at the familiar voice. "Good morning."

"If you say so," he replied. "Look, I've got a start on the Portland records and I'll send them to Bend. I called Eileen Hanna at the Bend office so she'll be expecting them. She didn't ask any questions when I said they were just some financial projections that you asked for."

"Good."

"However, she might get a little suspicious when she sees the volume of paper involved," John warned.

"Don't worry about it. I'm sure Eileen won't question anything that I want." Eileen was one of the few employees in the vast timber empire who didn't begrudge Ashley her inheritance. The quiet, fiftyish woman was a feminist to the end and perceived that any advance of women in the timber industry was a major step in the right direction.

"I'm still working on the rest of it. I'm afraid it will take a couple of weeks to pull all the records together."

"That's fine. I'm not as concerned with how long it takes as much as I am that we do a thorough job." When she replaced the receiver, she found that Trevor had entered the room and was leaning against the arch separating the kitchen from the den. He studied her lazily, sipping his coffee.

The thought that he was listening in on her telephone conversation with John made her bristle. "Are you trying to add eavesdropping to your skills of crime, Senator?" she asked scathingly. Her ragged emotions took hold of her in an uncharacteristic burst of anger. "First we have breaking and entering and now we can add eavesdropping. If you don't watch out, I might be inclined to believe that last summer's bribery charge wasn't phony after all."

The gentle smile that had curved his lips disappeared, replaced by a grim line of determination. The glint in his steely blue eyes became deadly and his jaw was tight with the restraint he placed upon himself.

"I came over here this morning because I thought that we could settle a few things between us," he stated flatly. "But obviously that's impossible."

Regret washed over her. "Look, I didn't mean—"

"It doesn't matter." He set his cup on the bookcase and stared at her with condemning eyes. "You never have trusted me and I doubt that you ever will. All your well-rehearsed speeches about being your own woman are a lot of garbage, Ashley. What it all boils down to is that you're afraid of men and me. You can't let yourself feel anymore."

His vehement words hit her like a blast of arctic air, chilling the kind feelings she had felt for him. She ignored the tears pooling in her eyes and leveled her disdainful sea-green gaze in his direction. "I was talking to John Ellis, the accountant for the timber company. He's doing some work for me—work that I requested because of you. In a couple of hours I can pick up the reports in Bend.''

His smile was forced and cynical. "Good. Then maybe you can find out just how misplaced your loyalties have been." He walked to the door and put his hand on the knob. "Call me when you find out whom Claud paid to do his dirty work!"

"If I do—"

Every muscle in his body tensed and his hand whitened over the doorknob. "Just remember that we have a deal, lady. I expect you to hold up your end."

A gust of cold air filled the room as he opened the door. He walked out and slammed the wooden door behind him. The tears that had been pooling in Ashley's eyes began to flow. "Damn you, Trevor Daniels," she whispered, her small fists clenching. "Why can't I just forget you?"

Managing to pull herself together, she walked across the room and picked up Trevor's empty cup from the shelf on which he had placed it. She started into the kitchen, but stopped, her green eyes focused on the table.

There, shining dully against the polished maple, was Trevor's key to the cabin.

Chapter Five

The office in Bend wasn't particularly large, but it was run efficiently due to Eileen Hanna's sharp eyes and knack for organization. When Ashley entered the airy offices located on Wall Street, Eileen looked up from her desk and smiled broadly.

"I've been expecting you," the plump, red-haired woman exclaimed as she led Ashley into a private office.

"It's good to see you again," Ashley replied with a good-natured smile. "If all the offices of Stephens Timber were run this efficiently, I'd be out of a job."

"Nonsense!" Eileen replied, but warmed under the compliment. She unlocked a closet, withdrew a neat stack of computer printouts and handed them to Ashley.

"John said you wanted to go over some projection figures. Looks like he got a little carried away."

"I told him to send me anything that might be pertinent," Ashley said, eyeing the reams of paper. "I guess he took me literally."

"He's an accountant, what do you expect?"

Ashley laughed. "What I expect is more printouts."

"You're not serious." Eileen withdrew a cigarette from her purse and tapped it on the corner of the desk.

"John said that he might be sending a few more things to me later today or tomorrow. I'll pick them up on Thursday."

"Maybe you should bring a semi," Eileen suggested as she lit her cigarette and blew a thin stream of smoke toward the ceiling.

"I'll keep that in mind." Ashley hoisted the neatly bound papers under her arm and smiled fondly at the industrious woman.

"Next time you're here, I'll buy you lunch."

"It's a date, but I'll buy," Ashley promised as she walked out of the room and winked broadly. "It's time I got some use out of my expense account." When Ashley left the building, she could still hear Eileen chuckling.

It had been difficult to keep thoughts of Trevor from interfering with her work. The harsh words of their final argument kept flitting through her mind. She had been unnecessarily cruel because of her conflicting emotions and now she regretted the fact that she had blown up at him. It had crossed her mind to call the Lambert house and apologize to Trevor, but she had discarded the idea for now. She wanted to review all the information she had received from John Ellis before talking with Trevor again. Besides, she figured she and Trevor each needed a little time to cool off.

During the following two days, Ashley studied every computer printout that John had sent. She wasn't happy with herself until she had looked over each entry and sifted through the documents with a fine-tooth comb. By the end of the second evening, Ashley had barely made a dent in the volumes of information sitting on the edge of the desk in the den. Her eyes were burning and her muscles ached from her cramped position of leaning over the desk.

The grandfather's clock had just struck eight when Ashley heard the rumble of an engine nearing the cabin. A pleased feeling of exhilaration raced through her body. Waiting, she removed her reading glasses and tapped nervous fingernails on the edge of the desk. The engine was cut and footsteps approached the cabin. Within seconds there was a loud knock.

With a satisfied smile, Ashley answered the door. Trevor stood on the porch wearing his enigmatic smile and tight, worn jeans. Snowflakes had collected in his dark hair and began to melt and catch the reflection of the interior lights. He was carrying a large package under his arms.

"If it isn't Senator Daniels?" Ashley teased.

"Not yet, it isn't," he replied. "Ask me again in November."

"Come in," Ashley requested, standing aside. She viewed him from beneath the sweep of dark lashes, and her green eyes gleamed wickedly. "Isn't it nice to have an invitation for once?"

His broad shoulders slumped, but his dark eyes glittered. "Why do you purposely goad me?" he asked in exasperation. "I came here with a peace offering, but I can see you're not in the mood to settle our differences."

"I doubt that we can do that in one night—"

"You might be surprised," he ventured, his voice lowering suggestively.

Ashley's interest was piqued. She couldn't hide the light of expectation in her round eyes. A pleased blush colored her cheeks. "Just what have you got in mind?"

"You'll see...." Trevor brushed past her and went into the kitchen. Ashley followed in his wake, barely able to conceal her interest.

"What have you got..." Her words died in her throat as he took off his jacket and unwrapped the ungainly package. Stripping the white paper away, he exposed two large Dungeness crabs. With a frown of approval, he placed the orange shellfish in the sink. "Where did you get those?" Ashley asked as she eyed the crabs speculatively.

"Newport."

"You drove clear to the coast and back?"

"It's only a few hours—don't you remember?"

She swallowed against the lump in her throat. "Of course I remember," she whispered hoarsely before turning away from him to hide the tears that were gathering in her eyes. The last time she had been with him, they had met in secret rendezvous near Neskowin on the rugged Oregon coast. All night long they had watched the stormy sea batter the rocky shoreline from the window of the small beach house. After dining on fresh crab and wine, Trevor had made erotic and endless love to her until the dawn had come and torn them apart.

"Come on, Ashley," he persisted, walking over to her and wrapping his arms around her waist. "Lighten up. Let's just try to forget the bad times and concentrate on the good."

"That might be easier said than done," she murmured.

He pressed a soft kiss into her blue-black hair. "Not if you try. Besides, it's Christmas Eve."

"I know." She had expected to spend the holiday alone for the first time in years and had tried to ignore the loneliness she felt. Now Trevor was with her and her spirits lifted.

"Then let's have a truce—in honor of the holiday."

"Okay, Senator," she said bravely, despite the churning emotions battling in her throat. "I'll give it a shot." Blocking out the storm of feeling raging within her, Ashley forced all of her attention on the simple tasks of heating French bread, tossing together a green salad and pouring the wine while Trevor cleaned and cracked the crabs. They worked in silence and Ashley was caught in memories of the past.

The light meal was enjoyable. Side by side, they sat by the fire in the den and laughed about the good times they had shared. Trevor was as charming as he had ever been and Ashley knew that if she let herself, she could fall hopelessly in love with him all over again. The rich sound of his laughter, the merry twinkle in his bright blue eyes and the sensual feel of his fingers when he would lightly touch her shoulder reminded her of the happiest time in her life—when she had been desperately in love with him. Even without all of the traditional trimmings, the evening became the warmest and happiest Christmas Eve she could remember. Relaxing with Trevor was perfect and natural.

Several hours had passed before Trevor cocked his head in the direction of the desk. "You've been looking over the records of Stephens Timber," he deduced.

"That's right. But I'm afraid you'll be disappointed. So far, everything looks fine. Nothing to prove that anyone in the family is the criminal you suspect."

"You're sure?" She felt him stiffen. He was sitting behind her on the floor, his strong arms folded securely over her shoulders. She was leaning against him as she stared into the glowing red embers of the fire.

She shook her head and her hair brushed against his chest. "I've barely started. Those reports are just for the last few months. I looked them over quickly and they seemed okay. I couldn't see anything glaringly obvious."

"Claud doesn't make glaring mistakes," Trevor stated. All traces of humor had disappeared from his voice.

"I know, I know. I've started going through the pages again. This time I'm studying each entry individually, but it's going to take weeks."

"Ashley." His fingers pressed urgently against her shoulders and dug into the soft muscles of her upper arm. "I don't have much time."

"Then I'm going to have to recruit help, Senator," she decided with a sigh. "I have other things I have to do. I can't spend the next two months sequestered with computer printouts just to uphold your good name."

"Or yours." He reminded her. "Just make sure your recruit is someone you can trust."

"Of course."

"This is important. Anyone who helps you can't tip Claud off. Can you be sure that the people working for you are loyal to you and not your cousin?"

Ashley didn't hesitate. "There are a few. Give me a break, Trevor. We employ over—"

"That doesn't matter. It's not quantity, but quality that counts."

"I can handle it."

"I hope so," he whispered, touching his lips to her hair. "Sometimes I question your judgment."

"That's the problem, isn't it? You always have."

The air was thick with unspoken memories. Silence weighed heavily on Ashley's slim shoulders as she stared into the bloodred coals of the fire. "I don't know you anymore, Trevor. Not at all," she said in a quiet moment of complete honesty. "And what I remember...what happened between us, turned out very badly." She turned her head and her green eyes looked directly into his.

"A man can change..." he ventured.

"And so can a woman."

His eyes searched the soft contours of her face before she turned away from him to concentrate on the slowly dying fire. "What if I said that I wish I had it all to do over again?" His fingers touched the round of her shoulders and lingered in the black silk of her hair.

The old ache burned savagely in her heart. "I'd say I don't believe you—no matter how much I'd like to. I'm not bitter, Trevor; just wiser than I was. What happened between us was your doing and nothing you can say will alter the past." She felt the warmth of his fingers in her hair and knew that she had to pull away from him and break the seductive spell he was weaving. She couldn't let herself forget the past and the pain. Struggling against reawakened love, she managed to stand and step away from the power of Trevor's touch.

Her voice was firm. "I think it would be better to forget what happened eight years ago and concentrate on what's happening now. For instance, the reason you're here and what you really want from me."

The grandfather's clock in the entry hall ticked off the silent seconds. A chill as cold as a North Pacific gale made Ashley shiver with dread and she rubbed her hands over her arms.

"I thought we could spend some time together. It's Christmas." Trevor's eyes never left her face. He watched even the most subtle of her reactions; the nervous manner in which she clutched the gold chain encircling her throat, and the movement of her tongue as she wet her lips. Desperately she wanted to believe him.

"And you need me to check into the company records to condemn my own family. Isn't that what this is all about? Isn't that the only reason you're here? Aren't you just trying to clear all the dirt surrounding the Daniels family and push it onto the name of Lazarus Stephens in order that you can get elected? That is the most important thing isn't it? Your career."

"And what's important to you, Ashley?" Trevor asked quietly. His face had saddened. "Eight years ago all you wanted to do was settle down, get married, have children. Now you're talking about women's rights and finding yourself! What the hell's that supposed to mean?" His blue eyes were blazing. "And what about your husband—how does he feel about all this new way of thinking? Or is he the reason you've become so liberated?"

Ashley's eyes snapped with indignation. "Richard and I were divorced four years ago."

"I know that."

"Then why do you continue to refer to him as my husband?"

"Because he was!"

"And that still bothers you," she said, understanding a little of his pain.

"Shouldn't it?" His cold blue eyes narrowed and he lifted himself from the floor, trying to relieve the tired muscles supporting his back.

"You were the one who couldn't make a commitment," she reminded him, hoping to hide the trace of wistful regret in her voice.

Trevor's fist opened and closed against his jeans, as if he were physically attempting to regain control of his temper. "Don't twist the truth," he warned. "I was willing to do just about anything to keep you—"

"Except marry me."

"Ha!" The sound of his humorless laughter was as bitter as the night. "How many times did I ask you to marry me? Or have you conveniently forgotten about them?" His voice was low, the sound dangerous. There was a kinetic energy in the air, ready to explode with the repressed passion of the heated argument.

Ashley's dignity wavered for an instant. "That's right, Trevor. You did ask me to marry you, several times." She waved the back of her slim hand in the air as if the number were insignificant. "But asking isn't the same as doing. I was tired of being engaged and tired of having an affair. I wanted to be your wife!"

"Correction," he interjected cruelly, his dark blue eyes burning with accusations. "You wanted to be anyone's wife. Even if it meant running back to the man your father had chosen for you."

"I loved you...." She sighed, tears pooling in her eyes with the painful admission. "Trevor, I loved you so much."

"Until you realized that I wasn't going to become a millionaire overnight. The daughter of Lazarus Stephens wasn't able to live without the comforts of wealth. You couldn't wait for me, could you?"

"Now who's twisting the truth?" she charged.

"Damn it, Ashley, this isn't getting us anywhere." His fist crashed into the warm rocks of the fireplace and then he swore, wincing against a sudden, blinding stab of pain.

Ashley's anger fled and was replaced by concern. "Are you all right?"

"I'm fine."

"Trevor." She touched his arm. For a moment her fingers brushed his wrist and his blue eyes sought hers, unspoken questions in their stormy depths. Her throat tightened. He rubbed his forehead before letting his head fall backward to stare at the open rafters supporting the roof. "Dear God, Ashley, I wish I understood you."

His plea sounded earnest. A lump formed in her throat when she considered what she might have shared with Trevor. Had she waited, as he had asked, would all of the happiness of their youth have blossomed into a deep, selfless love? Could they have shared their lives? Would she have eventually borne his children, comforted him when he needed her, shared his deepest agony?

As if he had read her mind, he asked the one question he had been avoiding for three days. "Why did you come here, to the cabin?"

She withdrew her hand and tears filled her eyes. "There were a lot of reasons—I needed a rest, there was work I could do here, I wanted to get out of the office, but there was something else," she admitted with a wry frown. "I came here because of you." Sea-green eyes met his. "It seemed that every time I turned around, I was reminded of you. Just a few weeks after Senator Higgins's death, your name became a household word. Then there were the bribery charges—the newspapers... television...you were everywhere.

"When Dad died, all I heard about was what damage you would do if you were elected. Now, just lately, your accident hit the front page. I couldn't get away from you." Her voice softened. "I thought that if I came here for a couple of weeks, I could think things out, sort out my feelings."

"And have you?"

Her smile was frail and filled with self-mockery. "I thought I had." Her lips pursed into a thoughtful pout. "Now I'm not so sure." Emotions she had thought long dead were reawakening. She couldn't help but remember the feel of his hands against her skin, or the way his eyes darkened in passion when she smiled suggestively.

The rustic room seemed to shrink and become more intimate. Ashley had to concentrate to keep her thoughts from wandering dangerously to a distant past.

He stared down at her, attempting to look past the innocent allure in her eyes. She had always been a puzzle to him, enigmatic and beguiling; the only woman he had ever let touch his soul. He had vowed never to make that mistake again, and he had been able to keep that silent promise to himself until tonight, when he gazed into the intelligent complexity of her eyes. At this moment he wanted her more desperately than he had ever wanted anything in his life. "Do you want me to stay?"

She didn't avoid his penetrating gaze. "Yes. I've missed you, Trevor." Giving up all the thin pretenses, she faced what she had tried to deny for eight solitary years. "I've missed you so badly."

He forced himself to look past the tears welling in her eyes. "Not badly enough to come back."

"I couldn't." She shook her head and fought the tears. "I think you understand that my pride wouldn't allow it."

"I've never been able to understand anything about you."

Standing, she faced him. "Only because you never really tried."

Slowly his strong arms encircled her waist and pulled her body gently to his. There was a restraint in his touch and torment in his gaze.

"I must be out of my mind," he muttered to himself as his head lowered and his lips brushed hers. The pressure of the kiss increased. Ashley sighed through parted lips at the power of his arms and the warmth of his mouth covering hers. The faint taste of wine passed from his lips to hers and the familiar taste brought back memories as bittersweet as the past they had shared together.

Her knees seemed to melt with the warm persuasion of his embrace. She touched him lightly on the shoulders and could feel the tightening of lean, corded muscles beneath her fingertips.

His tongue rimmed her lips before slipping between her teeth to explore the secrets of her mouth. It touched her familiarly, sliding seductively against the polish of her teeth.

Trembling with a wave of passion, her fingers dug into the firm flesh of his shoulders. The forgotten ache of womanly need uncoiled wantonly within her, forcing her blood to race wildly through her veins and pound in her ears. Her breathing became rapid and shallow. With each flickering touch of his supple tongue against hers, her desire for him increased and the uncontrollable yearning became more heated; a throbbing distraction demanding release.

He lifted his head from hers, but continued to press her body against his, letting her feel the taut rigidity of each of his muscles straining against his clothing. "I want you," he whispered hoarsely against her hair. It was a statement as honest as the cold mountain night. "I want you more than I've ever wanted a woman."

She swallowed against the dryness that had settled in her throat. "And I want you," she murmured.

His penetrating eyes studied the mystery of her. "With you it's more than passion or lust. It always has been."

Her heart nearly missed a beat. If only she could believe that he loved her...just a little. "You've always had a way with words, Trevor. That's why you've done so well in politics, I suppose."

"Are you accusing me of distorting the truth?" His voice was thick and slightly mocking. A hint of laughter danced in his eyes. Ashley was captivated by his smile— the slightly off-center grin she had grown to love that summer eight years before.

"Stretching the truth," she corrected.

"In order to seduce you?"

"To get your way."

"If I'd had my way with you, things would be a lot different between us." His fingers wrapped possessively over her wrist. "Do you have any idea what you do to me?"

"I just want...to be with you," she whispered, rising onto her toes and kissing his cheek. Softly she outlined the shape of his brows with the tip of her finger. Everything she did seemed so natural, just as it had in the past.

Trevor groaned with the frustration tormenting him. He noticed the innocence in her clear green eyes and the heat burning in his loins began to ache. "Ashley," he ground out, "I don't want you to do anything you might regret."

"I won't."

He clenched his teeth together and forcefully willed his passion aside. "What I'm trying to say is that you don't have to feel obligated to me."

"I don't, Trevor," she replied, showing just the hint of a dimple. "Not anymore."

Her hand pressed against his cheek and he could stand the bittersweet torment no longer. With a sensual movement, he turned his head and touched the tip of his tongue to her palm, letting the moist heat from his body flow into hers.

"Trevor..." she moaned, her voice fading into the night. "Oh, Trevor." She shuddered with the pain of ragged emotions, the same feelings she had been denying for eight agonizing years. His tongue created a moist path between her fingers and she felt as if her entire body were ignited by his warm touch. Her throat became dry, her voice a breathless whisper. "I've always loved you," she vowed.

"I want to know that you're mine," he said, steeling himself against the desire running rampant in his veins and the passion dominating his mind.

"I always have been."

"Ashley, don't. Don't lie to me. Not now."

"I'm not—"

"Prove it."

"If only I could," she wished.

"Let me make love to you." It was a simple request. His dark blue eyes bored into her, exposing the depths of his torment. Her feelings for him were dangerous. They entrapped her in the same words of love that had betrayed her in the past. His offer was tempting, yet she hesitated, afraid of losing herself to him as she had once before.

"There's nothing I want more," she admitted.

"But you're afraid."

"There's no future for us...." Her dark brows had pulled into a worried frown. With all of her heart she wanted to lie beside Trevor, to find the exhilaration once again of becoming one with him. But the old fears resurfaced.

"Shhh. Don't think about tomorrow." His fingers caught in the thick strands of her blue-black hair, pulling her head to his. For a delicious moment, his lips brushed over hers, lingering just a fraction of a second. "Let me love you, sweet lady," he whispered.

Her response was to let go of the fear and the pain of the past. Her surrender was complete. "Please," she murmured. Reaching upward she twined her fingers in his hair and turned her lips upward to accept the warm invitation of his mouth.

"It's been so long," he groaned as his lips pressed against hers and conveyed to her his overwhelming masculinity.

Her heart thudded irregularly with the urgency of his kiss. Desire, hot and fluid, crept up her veins as she felt his tongue meet hers. Without breaking the heated kiss, he shifted and lifted her off the floor to cradle her against his chest. Trevor began to carry her up the stairs to the loft.

"I can walk," she protested, thinking of his recent injury.

"Not a chance," he replied. "You might change your mind."

"Never." Tears of happiness welled in her eyes as she looked up at the angular face of the man she loved.

When he reached the top of the stairs, Trevor didn't hesitate. He strode across the small loft and dropped Ashley onto the bed, before lying beside her. The room was shadowed, but in the pale illumination from the skylight, Ashley could make out the masculine angles of his face.

She felt the touch of his hand as he caressed her cheek and she read the desire smoldering in the depths of his eyes. His fingers slid seductively down her throat to linger at the neckline of her sweater.

Closing her eyes, she leaned against him and let out a shuddering sigh when his fingers dipped below the ribbing at her neck to tentatively touch the swell of her breast. Her hands worked at the buttons of his shirt, letting it fall open to expose his solidly muscled chest. The bandage, a swath of white against his dark skin, reminded Ashley of the reasons he had come to the cabin, the reasons he was here with her now. Her fingers gently outlined the white gauze.

Slowly he lifted the sweater over her head. Shivering slightly when the cool air touched her skin, she was only aware that she wanted Trevor as desperately as she ever had. She needed him now, tonight. She was destined to lie in the shelter of his arms, feel the strength of his body straining against hers. And there would be no regrets. Tonight she belonged to Trevor alone.

He watched her silently, his warm hands touching her cool skin. She swallowed against the arid feeling in the back of her mouth when his hand cupped her breast. The ache within her burned more savagely. When his head lowered and he touched the flimsy fabric of her bra with his lips, she thought she would die in the sweet agony ripping through her. Her breasts pushed against the thin barrier of lace and silk as his tongue wet the sheer fabric and the cool night air caressed her skin. He groaned as his mouth captured the hidden nipple straining against the taut lace.

Ashley clutched his head against her, exhilarating in the torment of his lovemaking. Tears ran down her cheeks as he unclasped her bra and her breasts were unbound. His fingers moved in slow rhythmic circles over one nipple while his tongue rimmed the other.

"Oh, God, Trevor," she pleaded. "Make love to me, please make love to me."

His hands found the waistband of her jeans, and his fingers dipped deliciously close to her skin. She was unaware of the precise moment when he removed the rest of her clothes as well as his own. She was only conscious of the sweet torment heating within her, a wild tempest of passion only he could calm.

When at last he moved over her, she was rewarded by the feel of his firm muscles pressed urgently over her body. His bare legs, soft with dark hair, entwined with hers. His hands touched her rib cage as if he were sculpting her, and his lips, hard with passion and warm with desire, molded over hers. "Love me, Trevor," she cried, unashamed of her tears.

"I always have...." He lifted his head and gazed into her soft green eyes. Her dark hair was spread over the white pillow. He knew now what he had always suspected: Ashley Stephens was the most incredibly beautiful and intelligent woman he had ever met.

Burying his head in the soft curve of her neck, he claimed her in a sensuously slow union of his flesh with hers. The warmth within her began slowly to uncoil as he found that part of her he had discovered sometime in a stormy past. He tasted the salty tears of happiness that ran down her cheeks; he felt the heated moment of her submission and stiffened when her fingernails dug into the muscles of his back.

Ashley whispered his name into the night when the final moment of surrender brought them together and bridged the black abyss of eight lost years.

As his body fell against hers, he held her as if he expected her to vanish. The corded muscles of his arms offered the gentle assurance that he did love her and always had. If only Ashley could believe him. If only she could think that Trevor would never leave.

Chapter Six

Sunlight was streaming through the windows when Ashley opened her eyes on Christmas morning. She snuggled deep beneath the colorful patchwork quilt and felt the warmth of Trevor's body against her own. He made a low sound in the back of his throat and the arm draped possessively across her abdomen tightened before his even breathing resumed.

Ashley watched his dark profile against the stark white sheets. In slumber, some of the harshness had disappeared from his features; the tension that had been with him the last few days had faded with the night. The lines around his eyes had softened and the pinched corners of his mouth were relaxed. His hair fell over his eyebrows. Ashley lovingly brushed it out of his face while she pushed herself up on one elbow and stared down at the only man she had ever loved. *Why, Trevor,* she thought sadly, *why can't we live like this forever? Why do we continually do battle with each other?*

The quilt covering Trevor had slipped downward, exposing his chest to the cold morning air. Ashley's eyes followed the rippling lines of his muscular body to rest on the white gauze wrapped tightly over his torso. Gingerly she touched the bandage, frowning thoughtfully. Was it possible that Claud could have been responsible for Trevor's accident? It seemed unlikely, and yet Ashley knew that Claud could be cruel and ruthless if he felt cornered or threatened. And Claud had mentioned to Ashley that he considered Trevor's senatorial bid a direct threat to Stephens Timber. To what lengths would her bitter cousin go?

Her touch disturbed him. Trevor opened a sleepy blue eye and smiled when he saw that Ashley was already awake.

"You're a sight for sore eyes," he murmured. The hand that had been curved over the bend in her waist moved seductively upward until his thumb rubbed against her rib. "God, I could get used to this." He stretched before sitting next to her and looking into the incredible allure of her eyes. "Merry Christmas, Ashley," he whispered before bringing his face next to hers and pressing anxious lips to her mouth.

Slowly, he pushed her back against the mattress and let his weight fall carefully over her. Her breasts flattened with the welcome burden of him and slowly she slid her fingers up the solid muscles of his arms to rest on his shoulders.

When he raised his head, there was a trace of sadness in his gaze. "You don't know how long I've waited to wake up with you beside me," he admitted. A wistful look stole over her refined features. Trevor traced the disbelieving arch of her brow.

Ashley felt as if her heart had swollen in her throat. "You only had to ask," she whispered.

Something dangerous flickered in his gaze. "You were married," he reminded her.

"That was a long time ago."

Trevor lay over her, his supple body imprisoning hers against the bed. She didn't move or attempt to escape from the gentle bonds of his muscles flexed possessively over hers. As she gazed into his knowing blue eyes, Ashley realized that she could never love another man. Her marriage to Richard had been a mistake from the start and it was over before it had ever begun.

"I should never have let you go," Trevor whispered into the thick ebony silk of her hair. His body began to move rhythmically over hers, enticing the most delicious responses. Her heartbeat thudded irregularly in her chest. "I should have chased you down and forced you to marry me."

"You wouldn't have had to force me, Trevor. That was the one thing in the world I wanted."

"And the only thing that Lazarus Stephens's money couldn't buy."

She let out a ragged sigh and looked beyond him to the exposed rafters of the ceiling. Her breathing was becoming shallow and rapid. "Must we always argue?"

"I can think of better things to do...."

Her fingers tangled in his hair. "So can I."

Trevor lowered his head, his lips claiming hers in a kiss filled with passion and despair. His hands rubbed against her skin, softly caressing her body and making her blood warm as it ran through her veins.

The magic of his touch evoked the most primitive of responses within her. Liquid heat circulated and swirled upward through her body as she felt the firm muscles of his chest brush erotically across her breasts, teasing the dark nipples to expectant peaks aching with desire.

His lips touched and teased her, inflaming the wanton fires of passion to surge through her veins until she began to move beneath him. Her hands strayed downward, touching the rippling muscles of his back and outlining each tense sinew with her fingertips.

Trevor closed his eyes and groaned in helpless surrender. His hands began to knead her breasts and his knees impatiently parted her legs, testing her willingness by rubbing himself gently against her abdomen.

A soft gasp escaped from her throat, and when he lowered his head to capture her parted lips with his, Ashley thought she would die with wanting him. His tongue explored and plundered the sweet delights of her mouth while he gripped her shoulders firmly with his hands and entered the dark warmth of her womanhood.

Ashley's mind was swirling with erotic images. Her fingers dug into his back as she felt the womanly pressure within her build. Slowly, as if enjoying the torture of denial, he pushed closer to her, touching her most intimate core, closing the space that held her away from him and savoring the sweet agony of her cry.

"Please," she whispered throatily, her glazed eyes looking into his. Her throat was dry, the words a strain. "Take me, Trevor," she begged.

The light of satisfaction glimmered in his eyes as he began to thrust against her. He watched in fascination while she responded in kind, holding on to him in desperate need, as if she expected him to disappear into the cool morning air.

Sweat beaded on his brow and glistened against his naked skin as he restrained himself, waiting until he felt the warmth of her explode in a liquid burst of satiation. Then he, too, let go and felt the sudden rush of blinding fire as he sealed their union of flesh and mind and fell heavily against her with a moan of triumphant release.

"I love you, Ashley," he claimed. "God forgive me, but I've always loved you. Even when you were married to another man."

The lump in Ashley's throat expanded with his words. "Shhh, Trevor—not now." Lovingly, her fingers touched his hair, smoothing the wavy chestnut strands away from his face. His words touched the deepest, most precarious part of her heart and she couldn't allow herself the luxury of believing them. Not now. Not ever.

She had felt the pain of his betrayal once before and had sworn never to live the life of a fool again. It would be too easy to believe him—to trust her heart—to let the pain recapture her in its bittersweet claws.

After a few moments of reflective silence, Ashley attempted to lighten the mood in the cold cabin. "How about breakfast in bed?" she asked.

Trevor smiled knowingly and ran a sensuous finger down the length of her body. "I'm afraid I wouldn't be able to concentrate on food."

She laughed and shook her hair out of her eyes. "Well, I could. I'm hungry enough to eat a horse. Come on." Slapping him playfully on his rump, she hopped out of the bed, grabbed her robe and slipped it on. "I'll make breakfast while you get the fire going in the den."

"And then you'll serve me in bed?"

Ashley was halfway to the bathroom by the time his words hit her. When she turned to look over her shoulder and cast him an intentionally provocative glance, she found him leaning on one elbow, his blue eyes following her every move.

"You are talking about breakfast, aren't you, Senator?"

"Among other things..."

"Um-hmm. I think we'd better eat in the kitchen. It might be safer."

"Spoilsport."

"Look who's talking. You're the one with the important project, or have you forgotten?"

"It's Christmas!"

Ashley smiled despite herself. "That it is. Merry Christmas, darling." She winked at him seductively, turned on her heel and made a big show of going into the bathroom to change. She half expected him to follow her and was more than slightly disappointed when he didn't.

After she had showered and changed, she walked through the loft again and noted that he was still in bed, but far from sleeping.

"Come here," he commanded when she breezed past the four-poster. His delft-blue eyes were smoldering with passion.

"Not on your life," she teased, but when he reached out and took hold of her wrist, she was forced to spin around and face the determined set of his jaw. Her wet hair dangled in glistening ebony ringlets around her flushed face as he roughly pulled her down on the bed.

"You're no gentleman, Senator Daniels," she laughed as she fell against him.

"And you love it." His fingers toyed with the buttons of her sweater. "Someone should teach you a lesson, you know."

"And you're applying for the job?" Her eyebrows rose a skeptical fraction.

"I've got it." One of the pearllike fasteners near her neck was loosened, exposing just a hint of white skin at her shoulder. Her green eyes danced in mock dismay as she clutched at her throat. The love she had harbored for eight long years was unhidden in the even features of her face.

There was something captivating about Trevor's slightly off-center smile, something inviting and dangerous in his midnight-blue eyes. When he leaned over to kiss her shoulder, Ashley shuddered with anticipation.

He buried his face in her neck and drank in the sweet scent of her clean, damp hair. It held the faint fragrance of wildflowers, just as he remembered it. They had been alone in the cabin, and the dewy drops of summer rain had clung to her hair.

"I've never wanted a woman the way I want you," he admitted, touching her throat with his lips.

A thousand emotions made Ashley shiver as he pressed himself against her. She felt the ache of desire begin to flood her veins when he lay atop her and pressed the length of his naked body over hers. Even through her slacks and sweater she could feel the heat of his passion pressed urgently against her skin.

"Forget breakfast," he suggested, running his tongue against her ear. "I have a better idea...."

Without regret, Ashley wound her arms around his neck and brought his head against hers, eager to let the happiness linger and feel the warmth of his lips dispel the chill in hers.

As she poured water for coffee, Ashley could hear Trevor grumbling about the things he had to put up with. She smiled to herself when she remembered her hasty escape from the bed. After making glorious love while the late morning sun infiltrated the room through the skylight, she had dozed quietly in the shelter of Trevor's arms. Then, when she could tell that he wasn't expecting her to leave, she had bolted from the bed, snatched up her clothes from where they had been carelessly tossed and raced down the stairs to the kitchen.

He had sworn roundly, which had only caused her to laugh at his frustration. It felt so right, so natural being alone with him. It was almost as if what had separated them in the past was beginning to disappear.

While Trevor attended to the fire in the den, Ashley started preparing what she could for a festive brunch. The cupboards were pretty bare, but she prided herself on the end result of broiled grapefruit, blueberry muffins, sausage and poached eggs.

"Not too bad for a novice," she decided as she dusted her hands on the apron she had tied over her clothes.

Trevor must have heard her. "It's Christmas, you know. I'm expecting baked ham, cinnamon rolls, eggs Benedict...." He poked his head into the kitchen.

"Keep it up, Senator, and you'll be lucky if you get cornflakes."

He studied the floor for a minute before his eyes came back to rest on her. "It wouldn't matter what we ate, you know."

She returned his grin. "I suppose not. But since I put out the effort, I expect you to do the meal justice."

They ate in the kitchen and Trevor, for all his protests earlier, ate with relish. A surprised glint surfaced in his blue eyes. "I didn't think Lazarus Stephens's daughter knew how to boil water, let alone cook."

"I'm learning," she joked, before adding more seriously, "There are a lot of things you don't know about me, Trevor. I've grown up in the last eight years." He lifted his dark brows appreciatively, as if in mute agreement, and took a long swallow of his coffee.

The intimate conversation made Ashley bold. "So why haven't you ever married?" she asked before her courage escaped her.

He set his cup down and stared out the window for what seemed an eternity. "I'd like to give you the old cliché about never finding the right woman," he replied, rubbing his chin in the process and continuing to stare at the frosty panes. "But then, we both know it would be a lie."

Ashley stared at him, her breath caught in her throat. She shook her head sadly. "I just told you that I've grown up. I'm not as naïve as I was, Trevor, nor as—"

"Trusting?"

"That, too, I suppose. I'd like to think that you and I were just star-crossed lovers and that our time hadn't come yet. Now that we've found each other again, everything will be fine." She ran one finger around the rim of her cup and stared at the murky coffee. Her voice had grown hoarse. "But that's not the way it is. You're not Prince Charming, and I'm certainly no Sleeping Beauty, waiting for a man to change my life." Her sea-green eyes held his calmly. "Too much has happened between us. And," she added pointedly, "it's my guess that the reason you haven't married is that you haven't found the perfect mate."

"Is there such a thing?"

"I doubt it." She shook her head. "You want too much in a wife, Trevor. A strong woman, who will support you and your damned career. A woman who will do what you want without question, but still has a mind of her own. A woman who will give up everything to be at your side—if and when you want her. And a woman who will wait with the home fires burning until you decide to come home. That's too much to expect from anyone."

"Including you."

She smiled sadly. "Especially me."

"And what do you want in a husband?"

Love, she thought to herself, but couldn't force the word from her lips. Instead, her lips puckered into a secretive frown and she started picking up the dishes. "I don't want a husband," she replied.

"You did once. Very badly, as I recall."

"That was a long time ago."

He scowled darkly and his fingers drummed angrily on the table. "And you managed to get yourself one, didn't you?"

"It didn't last."

"Why not?"

She shrugged her shoulders to indicate that it really didn't matter, but Trevor's fingers gripped her forearm and restricted her movements. "Richard and I weren't suited—"

"That's a lie! The man was hand-picked by your father."

"Maybe that was the problem." She looked pointedly at her wrist and the tanned fingers restraining it.

With obvious reluctance Trevor let go of her arm. "This isn't getting us anywhere," he muttered, pushing back his chair before fiercely striding out of the room. Ashley heard his footsteps echo in the hall before the front door of the cabin opened, only to slam shut with a resounding thud that rattled the timbers of the rustic mountain retreat.

Knowing that it would be best to let him cool off, Ashley finished clearing the table and set the dishes in the sink to soak before grabbing her jacket from the hall tree, slipping on her boots and going outside.

Trevor's footprints left deep impressions in the snow. She followed the powdery prints and forced her hands deep into her pockets. She loved Trevor with a passion that was achingly evident every time she was near him, and yet, try as she would, she could find no way of resolving those problems that held them apart.

When she found Trevor he was standing near the edge of a sharp ravine, his back to her. He was staring past the snow-covered abyss to the majestic peaks beyond. The sky was a brilliant blue and the snow-laden mountains stood proudly in the distance, their treeless upper slopes reflecting the icy radiance of the winter sun's rays.

Trevor hadn't heard her approach and when Ashley put a reproachful hand against his sleeve, he stiffened. "I didn't mean to pick a fight, you know," she whispered, her breath misting in the cold mountain air.

His smile was cynical, and a muscle worked beneath his clean-shaven jaw. "Seems like you and I can't avoid arguing."

"It's hard to clear the air."

"Especially when so many lies cloud it." He thrust his fists deep into his pockets and leaned against the denuded white trunk of a birch tree. Thoughtfully he pursed his lips and his dark brows drew together in careful consideration over intense blue eyes.

"I never have lied to you," she replied.

He looked as if he didn't believe her. "But your family. First Lazarus, now Claud—"

"My family would never have come between us," she replied, "if you weren't so hell-bent to ruin Stephens Timber Corporation."

A sound of disgust formed in his throat. His eyes had turned as frosty as the winter day. "You can't convince me that Claud isn't out to get me."

"I know. I've tried."

"He's out to ruin me politically, Ashley."

"I think you're jumping to conclusions."

"The right ones. Claud is scared spitless that if I win I'll be able to lobby for wilderness protection and somehow cut off his supply of timber. Your father was opposed to any new wilderness protection acts. He didn't give a damn about the environment, and it seems as if Claud was tutored well."

"But Claud doesn't own the company."

"No, he just runs it. And he won't rest until he's ruined me politically."

"That's ridiculous!" Ashley retorted. She brushed the snow from a boulder and sat on it, holding her knees with her arms and huddling for warmth. Try as she might, she couldn't believe that Claud would be so murderous. It was true that Trevor's campaign included a firm stand on wilderness protection, which, in the past, Stephens Timber had vehemently opposed. The issue was a delicate one, pitting the economy against the environment. In lean times, when unemployment was high, jobs and the timber industry won over the environment. But right now, unemployment was down and public sentiment seemed to support Trevor's position.

"Senator Higgins was an efficient lobbyist for the timber industry," Trevor said. His broad shoulders slumped as if he were bone-tired.

"And you won't be?"

"Right. Higgins was in your father's pocket and I suspect that Claud is hoping that another candidate will fill Higgins's shoes." Trevor's voice was without inflection, but his face was a study in grim resolve. "He can look somewhere else because it sure as hell won't be me."

Ashley smiled bitterly. "I don't see where you get off acting so sanctimonious. Your family is still a very viable force in the timber industry."

"But my brother keeps his nose clean."

"What's that supposed to mean?" Ashley demanded.

"Just that Jeremy has managed to follow pretty closely in my father's footsteps. Daniels Logging Company has always worked within the law."

"And my father didn't? Is that what you're implying?"

"I'm just stating the facts," he replied coldly. "Jeremy has seen to it that Daniels Logging has been ahead of its time. We've never clear-cut, always participated in reforestation, even before it was fashionable, and always left a buffer zone near streams, to protect the rivers." Trevor's square jaw hardened. "And to my knowledge, the use of pesticides by Daniels Logging has been kept to a minimum, in order to protect the public."

Ashley's elegant brows raised scathingly. "You've implied some pretty heavy charges, Senator."

"I've always called·'em as I see 'em."

"Or so your campaign manager would like the public to think."

Trevor scowled angrily, but didn't offer a rebuttal. He noticed the bluish tint to Ashley's lips and reluctantly he stood. After brushing the wet snow from his jeans, he said, "I think we'd better go back inside before you freeze to death."

"Are you worried about me—or the scandal my demise would cause?"

Trevor's admonishing stare was stern. "I wish for once, just once, you'd give me a break."

"That works two ways, you know."

They walked back to the cabin in silence, each wrapped in secret thoughts of the past that linked them, bound them together, and always kept them at sword's length from each other.

In some respects, Trevor was right, Ashley decided. Daniels Logging had always had an untarnished reputation for working with the government, its employees and the environmentalists, instead of opposing them. While Stephens Timber was forever being gossiped about for being ruthless and unsympathetic to both employees and the public, Daniels Logging was considered a cornerstone of Oregon industry.

Ashley gritted her teeth in determination. All that was about to change. Then both Trevor Daniels and Claud Stephens would understand what it meant to deal with her. She intended to make Stephens Timber a model company, come hell or high water.

Ashley's thoughts were grim, but she had trouble believing that Claud would actually try to force Trevor out of the campaign, either by the phony bribery charges or this last, unbelievable mishap with Trevor's car. Claud was too much of a coward to do anything so bold. It wasn't his style to take unnecessary risks. And none of the records indicated foul play, at least she hadn't found anything out of the ordinary.

Ashley breathed a silent prayer begging that her instincts about her cousin were right.

Once back in the cabin, she managed to steer the conversation in any direction but on Trevor's career or the past. Trevor seemed to be taking pains to avoid another argument as well. The afternoon faded slowly into nightfall.

It wasn't a traditional Christmas by any standards. No candles, roast goose, lighted tree or carolers gave the holy day the special traditions Ashley had observed in the past. However, being alone in the mountains, wrapped in the strong arms of the one man who had ever meant anything to her, made this Christmas more special and intimate than any she could remember celebrating. What better way to observe the holiday than to share it with the man she loved with all her heart?

That night, lying in the security of Trevor's embrace, listening to the regular beating of his heart as he slept, Ashley cried soft tears of quiet happiness and whispered a silent prayer of gratitude for the special moments she had shared with him.

The cabin was illuminated only by the glowing, blood-red embers of the fire and the pale moonglow reflecting on the soft blanket of snow outdoors. The paned windows were frosted from the cold and the only sound breaking the stillness of the night was the occasional hiss of the fire as it encountered pitch.

Ashley closed her eyes and tried not to think that this night might be the last she would ever spend with him.

The sharp ring of the telephone brought Ashley out of a deep and trouble-free sleep. Trevor groaned, shifted on the bed and then continued to snore peacefully without even opening an eye. The last few weeks had exhausted him.

Carefully, so as not to disturb him, Ashley slipped from beneath the covers, grabbed her robe and hurried down the stairs to answer the phone in the kitchen. As she picked up the receiver, she pushed the tangled strands of her hair out of her eyes.

"Hello?"

"Ashley!"

With a sinking sensation, Ashley recognized the smug male voice of her cousin. "Good morning, Claud," she replied quietly, careful not to awaken Trevor. After sneaking a careful glance up the stairs, she walked to the far side of the small room, stretching the telephone cord its full length.

"What's going on?" Claud demanded after a few strangling moments of silence.

"What's going on?" she repeated casually, though her heart had seemed to miss a beat. She knew in an instant that Claud was on to her plan to help Trevor. "What do you mean?"

"Knock it off, Ashley. I know that you've been checking up on me."

Ashley's nerves were stretched to the breaking point. She had to support herself by leaning a slim and sagging shoulder against the wall. Somehow, despite the dread constricting her throat, she managed to keep her voice steady.

"Of course I have. You've known that all along. That's why I quit my job. I decided that Stephens Timber needed me."

"So why are all the reports being sent to the Bend office?" Claud asked in a voice filled with gruff indignation. "It looks to me like you're doing a major audit of the books."

"I told you I wanted to check all of the records," she replied evenly.

"There's more to it than that," Claud accused. Ashley could almost hear the wheels turning in his mind.

"Just a simple, all-encompassing audit."

"We have accountants to do that."

"I prefer to look over everything myself."

"You can stop whitewashing, Ashley. I know you're up to something. I just want to know what it is."

"Nothing all that mysterious, Claud. I just want to personally examine the books."

"In Bend? Over Christmas? Give me a break, for Christ's sake. You're supposed to be on a vacation."

"I am."

"With the company records?" He was clearly dubious.

"Right."

"You sure know how to have a good time," he mocked, openly challenging her.

Ashley smiled grimly to herself. "I'm not the kind of person to shirk my responsibilities, Claud. You may as well face that fact right now. Either you can work with me or against me, but we both know who makes the ultimate decisions regarding the company."

"And you just love to rub my nose in it, don't you?" Claud said disgustedly.

"Only when I'm forced to." She let out a weary sigh of frustration and tried to assuage her cousin's growing suspicions. "Look, Claud, what I'm doing is merely routine. Now that my job with the college is over, I think I should spend as much time as possible acquainting myself with the company books. Otherwise I won't be all that effective, will I?

"I intend to be more than just a figurehead with this corporation. It's my duty to learn everything there is to know about Stephens Timber."

"So you called John Ellis? Why didn't you get in touch with me?"

Nervously she twisted the phone cord, but she forced her voice to remain determined. "I did. Remember? You were the one who balked at sending me the information I needed."

"So you went behind my back."

"I did what I had to do."

Claud was still angry, but his suspicions seemed to be placated, at least for the moment. "So when will you be in Portland?" he asked, changing the subject.

"Soon. I don't have a precise date, but sometime before the first of the year." Ashley wanted to end the conversation as quickly as possible, before Trevor woke up. "I've got things to do right now, but I'll talk to you when I'm back in town. I'm sure you'll be interested to know how the books look."

"I already do," Claud muttered before hanging up.

When Ashley replaced the receiver, she let out a long sigh of relief and turned toward the stairs. She found herself face-to-face with Trevor. His expression was murderous.

"So someone at Stephens Timber tipped Claud off," he charged.

Ashley stood her ground, refusing to back down to the anger in the set of his jaw. "Claud's suspicious, if that's what you mean."

"What I mean, dear lady," Trevor spat out, "is that no one in that damned timber company of yours can keep his mouth shut." A deadly gleam of anger sparked in his eyes. "Or else you were just stringing me along all the time. This entire meeting was just a charade."

"I didn't come knocking on your door," Ashley pointed out, her eyes widening in disbelief.

"But you didn't exactly fight me off, did you?" he threw back at her, his angry glare burning through to her soul.

A small part of Ashley wanted to wither and die. Could this be the same man she loved with all of her heart? Did he really believe that she had sold him out? The fists rammed against his hips and the tense muscles straining beneath his shirt indicated that he was barely holding on to his temper, as if he really thought she had betrayed him.

"I wanted to be with you, Trevor."

"Why?" he demanded, taking a step nearer to her and gripping her shoulders with his tense fingers. "Why? So that you could get close to me? Are you just like the rest of your family, Ashley? Would you do anything to protect your name?" he asked, his words slicing through her heart as easily as a razor.

"Of course not!"

"No?" Disbelief contorted his rugged features. His eyes narrowed in unspoken accusation. "You didn't believe a word I said, did you? And you had no intention of holding up your end of the bargain."

"You know better than that," she insisted, her words trembling as they passed her lips. Dread slowly inched up her spine.

"What I know is that you used me, lady. You slept with me just so you could get close—see how I planned my campaign—so that you could protect your timber empire."

Ashley was too numb to speak. The fingers pushing into her flesh were painful, but not nearly as agonizing as the words coming from Trevor's lips.

"You missed your calling, lady," he stated. "You should have been an actress. That performance you gave me last night was damned near convincing!"

Without thinking, she raised her hand as if to slap him, but the fingers tightening on her shoulders prevented the blow from landing.

"You bastard," she hissed, tears beginning to run down her face.

"Like I said before—I call 'em as I see 'em."

"Then you're a blind man!" She pulled herself free of his grasp, lifting her head above the treachery of his insults. "You never could believe that all I ever wanted was you. You never could trust me and you never will."

A muscle worked at the corner of his jaw. For a moment the anger on his face was replaced by raw and naked pain. But just as quickly as it had appeared, his misery was hidden and Trevor's blue eyes became as cold as the midnight sun.

"Just remember that you and I have a bargain, lady. I expect you to keep your end."

She took in a shuddering breath. "And if I don't? What will you do, Trevor?"

"I swear to you that I'll destroy Stephens Timber Corporation and drag your family's name through the mud until it will never come clean."

"So much for the image of the kind and just politician," she threw back at him. "You'd better watch out, Senator, that gilded reputation you work so hard to keep in the public view might just become tarnished."

"I don't give a damn about my reputation, Ashley, and you know it."

"What I know is that nothing matters to you—nothing other than your damned career. That's all it's ever been with you, Trevor." His head snapped upward, as if she'd struck him. "I was foolish enough to think that you cared for me once," she continued, unable to stop the words from tumbling from her lips. "But now I'm a little older and wiser."

He looked as if he was about to protest. His broad shoulders sagged and he shook his head, as if he couldn't stand to hear another word. "If only you knew," he whispered.

"I'll keep up my end of the bargain," she stated wearily, "just to prove you wrong."

He managed a bitter smile before he turned toward the door. She stood in the hallway, unable to move, her arms cradled protectively over her breasts, and watched in miserable silence as Trevor slowly pulled on his boots, buttoned his jacket and placed an unsteady hand on the door.

"Good-bye, Ashley," he whispered, casting one last glance over his shoulder in her direction.

She couldn't even murmur his name. Her throat was hot and swollen with the grief of losing him again. In an instant he was gone, leaving her cold and bereft, just as he had done nearly eight years ago....

She slumped to the floor totally alone and surveyed the cabin with new eyes. Was this the place, the very spot, where her love for Trevor had begun?

The tears ran down her face in earnest as she remembered the first time she had ever laid eyes upon the ruggedly handsome face of Trevor Daniels.

Chapter Seven

Eight years ago, at the age of twenty-four, Ashley had been aware of the vicious rivalry between Stephens Timber and Daniels Logging. The rumors surrounding her father and some of his business practices couldn't be completely ignored, although Ashley chalked most of the gossip up to envy. Lazarus Stephens was a man of wealth and power. That was enough to start the eager fires of gossip running wild throughout the Oregon timber industry.

After she had graduated from a university in Paris, Ashley had taken a job with her father's company. In the year since she had started with the firm, she had held several positions; it had been apparent from the start that Lazarus was grooming his only child for the presidency of Stephens Timber, if—and when—he decided to retire. Ashley had been only too willing to follow in her father's footsteps. The only person who'd seemed to mind at all was her cousin Claud, who had been with Stephens Timber for several years and was jealous of his younger cousin.

Though she didn't like to admit it, Ashley realized that she had been spoiled beyond reproach by her overly indulgent father. Lazarus had lavished Ashley with anything she wanted after her mother's death. Expensive schooling abroad, flashy European sports cars, exotic vacations anywhere in the world; nothing had been too good for Lazarus's only child.

The end result was that Ashley had grown up pampered and expected to be treated like a princess. In a word, she was spoiled. And at twenty-four, it had begun to bother her. Her conscience had begun to twinge, if only slightly.

On her first vacation since starting to work with the company, Ashley decided to cancel her planned Mediterranean cruise, and instead, she spent her free time at her father's rustic cabin in the Cascade Mountains not far from Bend. For the first time in her life, Ashley began to recognize that the world didn't revolve around her or Stephens Timber. The glamorous life she had heretofore led began to lose its luster and appeal.

Even the image of her father was beginning to dim. She told herself that she had overheard too many idle tongues wagging, but she couldn't shake the feeling that something wasn't quite right with all of Lazarus's business dealings. Though she was loath to admit it, Ashley was beginning to wonder about the truth in the rumor surrounding Robert Daniels's disappearance. It was one subject her father avoided like the plague. He would never discuss anything to do with Robert Daniels or what had come between Lazarus and the man who had once been his business partner. Not even with Ashley. At the mention of Robert Daniels's name, Lazarus would visibly pale and then gruffly dismiss the subject. For the past year, ever since she had left the security of school abroad, Lazarus's animosity toward Robert Daniels had begun to make Ashley uneasy. She needed time to think things out and reevaluate her pampered life. And so, at the first opportunity, Ashley took off for the mountains.

The solitude of the rustic retreat made her depend solely upon herself for the first time in her life. The cabin hadn't been used since the summer before and smelled musty. As soon as she had changed into faded jeans, Ashley opened the windows, aired the rooms, washed the linen and scrubbed floors feverishly. No job was too difficult. She stacked wood in the garage and washed windows inside and out. At night her muscles ached, but she fell into a restless sleep with a feeling of vast accomplishment.

For the first week, she spent all of her time at the cabin either cleaning, experimenting in the rustic kitchen, reading or riding the horses that her father kept on the place. Zach Lambert usually took care of the two geldings, but while Ashley was staying at the cabin, she looked after the horses, much to Zach's obvious disapproval.

It was the second weekend since she had come to the mountains when the trouble began. Zach's daughter, Sara, who had been a childhood friend of Ashley's, insisted that Ashley come to a party Sara was hostessing for some of her friends from college. Ashley wasn't in the mood for a party and didn't want to attend, but found the prospect of spending another afternoon by herself just as dull. Besides, Ashley rationalized, there wasn't a polite way of declining. The Lambert place was just up the lane, and both Sara and her parents knew that Ashley was alone. There was no choice but to attend the party and hope for the best.

Ashley walked into the Lambert cabin knowing she had made a big mistake. The only person she recognized was Sara, and as hostess, Sara was dashing in and out, from one knot of jeans-clad guests to another. She smiled and waved to Ashley before hurrying into the kitchen to replenish a tray of hors d'oeuvres.

Ashley wandered through the modern cedar cabin and captured the attention of more than one pair of appreciative male eyes. In her backless apricot sundress, with her long black hair flowing loosely past her shoulders, she looked the part of a rich man's daughter.

Her green eyes moved over the other guests with cool disinterest, the smile on her face well practiced but vague. She wondered why she had accepted the invitation to the party at all and hoped she could find a viable excuse to leave the festivities early and return to the solitude of her father's cabin. She needed time alone to think about her life, her father and the business.

She accepted a glass of wine before edging toward the sliding glass door leading to the back of the cabin. Feeling the need to escape from the laughter and thick cigarette smoke, Ashley slipped out of the cabin and away from the crowd.

When she stepped onto the deck, a tall, broad-shouldered man approached her. He was older than she, but probably not yet thirty. His face was handsome, if somewhat angular, and his eyes were the deepest shade of blue she had ever seen.

He studied her intently, not bothering to hide his interest. Ashley experienced the disturbing feeling that she should recognize him. There was something familiar about him that made her uneasy.

The set of his mouth was slightly cynical for so young a man, and a few soft lines etched his forehead, giving him a wiser, more worldly appearance than could be expected for a man his age. His thick hair ruffled slightly in the wind and Ashley noticed that the chestnut color was streaked with gold—as if this man spent many hours in the sun.

Probably a cowboy, she thought to herself, glancing at his worn jeans and boots.

He stopped a few feet from her and leaned against the railing of the deck, supporting himself with his elbows as he stared brazenly at her.

"Is there something I can do for you?" she asked, tossing her wavy black hair behind her shoulders.

His thoughtful eyes narrowed. "Do I know you?"

"There's an original line," she retorted.

"It's not a line."

"Then, I doubt it." Ashley was sure that she would remember such a proud, defiant face.

A glimmer of recognition flashed in his eyes. "You're Ashley Stephens," he stated, as if the name meant something to him.

"And you're..." She lifted her dark brows expressively, begging his indulgence.

"Trevor Daniels."

Ashley's smile fell from her face. The name hit her like a ton of bricks. She was standing face-to-face with Robert Daniels's son. Though she had never met him, she had seen pictures that had been taken years ago. All the whispered innuendos she had heard about her father flitted through her mind. She swallowed back the sickening feeling rising from her stomach.

"I think it's about time we got to know each other," Trevor stated, his calm belied by an angry muscle working overtime near the back of his jaw.

"Why?"

"Because we have so much in common, you and I."

She looked disdainfully up at him. "I doubt that."

"Sure we do. Let's start with our fathers. Weren't they in business together once?"

"If you'll excuse me," Ashley whispered, taking a step away from this formidable man.

"I don't think so." A hand, large, powerful and surprisingly warm, reached out and took hold of her arm, spinning her back to face him. "I want to talk to you."

"About what?"

His face drew into a vindictive scowl. "Let's start with what you know about my father."

Other guests had joined them on the deck and were showing more than casual interest in the confrontation between Trevor Daniels and the attractive, raven-haired woman. Ashley's gaze flickered to the unfamiliar faces before returning to Robert Daniels's angry son. "I don't know anything about him," she whispered.

"But your father does."

Her eyes turned frigid. "I'm not interested in causing a scene, Mr. Daniels."

"I'll bet not."

"Then maybe we could drop this discussion."

"Not on your life."

"I have no idea what my father does or doesn't know about your family."

"Tell me about it."

Once again she glanced at the interested eyes trained upon her. "Not here!" She jerked her arm away from his grasp with as much pride as she could muster.

"Where then?"

He crossed his arms over his chest and eyed her speculatively. That intense, midnight-blue gaze started at her feet and inched up her body, appraising her. By the time his eyes had returned to hers, Ashley felt the stain of unwanted embarrassment burn her cheeks. "Let's talk about this in private."

"Anywhere you suggest," he agreed with a sarcastic curve of his sensual lips.

She had to think quickly. Guests had crowded the small Lambert cabin. Ashley was sure that there was no privacy anywhere in the house. "My father has a cabin...not far from here. After the party..."

"Now!"

She was about to protest but the hardening of his jaw convinced her that he meant business. After hasty apologies given to a slightly confused Sara, Ashley left the Lambert cabin with Trevor Daniels, his boots crunching ominously on the gravel, striding behind her.

Without an invitation, or so much as a look in her direction, Trevor got into the passenger seat of her sporty Mercedes convertible and for the first time in her life, Ashley was embarrassed by the ostentatious display of wealth.

The short drive was accomplished in stilted silence. Only the dull whine of the engine and the tires spinning on loose gravel disturbed the quiet of the mountains.

Ashley roared to a stop near the garage, pulled on the emergency brake and shut off the engine. "We can talk here," she suggested, but Trevor was already getting out of the car.

Damn the man! He intended to go inside. Just the thought of being alone with him made Ashley's pulse quicken. She chalked it up to the fact that he was Robert Daniels's son. That alone made her nervous.

Her hands were shaking when she unlocked the door, opened it and silently invited him inside.

Once in the den, Trevor looked at the less-than-opulent surroundings with a cynical arch of his brow. "Spending a quiet vacation in the mountains?" he mocked, his skeptical gaze taking in the interior before returning to her.

"I was."

"A change of pace from your usual style," he observed as he walked across the rustic room and stood near the window, pretending interest in the view of the craggy slopes of Mount Washington. He placed a boot on a footstool and leaned on one elbow as he studied the view. His jeans stretched tightly over his hips and thighs and Ashley had to look away from the erotic pose. Was it intentional? For a moment she wondered if he intended to seduce her, but pushed the rash thought aside. He seemed like a rational man, not one who might seek revenge against her father by compromising her.

But if he did, how would she react? The thought quickened her heartbeat. Trevor turned to look at her and Ashley realized he expected her to reply to his comment.

"How would you know what my usual style is?" she asked, her throat uncommonly dry.

Trevor grinned cryptically before moving away from the window and settling into one of the worn leather chairs near the empty fireplace. "There's a lot I know about you," he admitted, watching the slightly confused knit of her brow. "I know that you studied art in Marseilles before switching majors and universities, that you prefer BMWs to Chevys, that you would rather shop in San Francisco than L.A., and that you don't, for the most part, spend time alone in the Cascades."

Ashley listened to his observations with her breath catching in her throat. Either he was incredibly lucky at first impressions or he had spent a lot of time studying her. It occurred to her that their meeting at the Lamberts' wasn't by chance.

She gambled. "So why did you come looking for me?"

He didn't deny it. "I wanted your help."

She was wary. Her elegant brow puckered suspiciously. "But why?"

"I want to find out what happened to my father."

"I have no idea where he is," she replied honestly.

He thought for a minute, but seemed to believe her. His broad shoulders slumped slightly and he changed the subject, convinced that he would get no further with Lazarus Stephens's stubborn child. "So what are you doing up here, anyway?" Once again his merciless eyes traveled over the interior of the room, lingering for just a moment on the book Ashley had been reading. He picked it up and frowned. It was written in French. *"Les Misérables."* He looked at her sharply. "What're you trying to do—see how the other half lives?"

"Improve my mind," was her pert retort. Suddenly she wanted him out of the cabin and out of her life. There was something enigmatic and dangerous about him, something that touched her and wouldn't let go....

"Why did you come here?" he demanded, blue eyes seeking hers.

"I needed a vacation."

"You work for your father."

"That's right." How much did he know about her? Why did he care?

Trevor glanced from her to the loft, and back again. His fingers were tight with tension when he pushed them through the coarse strands of his hair. "It just doesn't fit," he muttered.

"What doesn't?"

"You...this..." He held up the book, making a sweeping gesture to include everything in the cabin. Finally, somewhat defeated, he returned his gaze to her. "You're not exactly what I expected."

"Sorry to disappoint you," she replied, noticing the hardening of his angular jaw. "Maybe you should have done your homework a little better."

He slowly rose from the chair and walked back to the middle of the room where she was standing. "I hate to admit it, lady," he whispered, "but you haven't disappointed me at all." He reached out. The tips of his fingers trailed the length of her bare arm, sending chills of anticipation through her veins, before lingering at her wrist.

"I haven't been much help to you."

"Yet." He stepped closer, and his gentle fingers didn't release her wrist. He tugged on her arm, bringing her body next to his. Ashley knew that he was about to kiss her and that it was madness, but the thrill of it all—the excitement of his touch—made it difficult to resist.

For a heart-stopping moment, she felt his hesitation, as if he, too, was unsure. "This can't happen," he whispered just before his lips pressed urgently against hers.

Ashley closed her eyes and swallowed against the persuasive warmth his kiss inspired. His fingers caught in the strands of her hair, holding her close, brushing against the exposed muscles of her back, begging for more intimacy. She felt her body, as if ripe with need, respond to him.

His fingers splayed against her naked back, forcing her closer to him. The gentle pressure of his chest crushing against her breasts created a savage fire that burned bright in the deepest part of her.

Her breasts ached for his touch and when an exploratory hand cupped the restrained fullness, she lifted her arms upward and wound them around his neck, thus offering more of herself to him. *This is crazy*, her mind screamed from somewhere in the dim reaches of her rational thoughts, but she couldn't stop the torrid fires beginning to consume her.

His head lowered and his lips nuzzled the exposed length of her throat, leaving in their wake a dewy path of desire. He kissed the hollow of her throat, his lips hovering over the sensitive pulse in soft warm breaths. Ashley responded, her heartbeat quickening convulsively.

Slowly, he pressed on her shoulders, forcing her to kneel with him. Then, when she was positioned to his liking, he lifted his head from her neck and gazed steadily into her eyes, watching her reaction as he leisurely slipped the thin strap of her halter dress over her left shoulder. She shuddered in anticipation, but continued to hold his gaze.

The dress fell open and one breast spilled out of the soft apricot fabric. Ashley felt an embarrassed blush rise upward through her body as Trevor gazed at her, his blue eyes fierce with desire. Tenderly his fingers came forward and traced the straining dark peak.

Ashley inhaled deeply, closing her eyes against the warm sensations swirling within her. How could one man make her feel as if she would do anything he commanded? She told herself that she was being reckless, playing with fire, but she didn't care. All she could think about was wanting him, a wild lust that was traveling in wicked circles within her body, aching for release.

"I've wanted you for a long time," he admitted, his voice rough. He was half lying now, and the warmth of his breath fanned her breast.

"You...you don't even know me...."

"That's where you're wrong, sweet lady. I've known you for so long, so very long."

"Just because I'm Lazarus Stephens's daughter."

His blue eyes were wicked when he looked up at her. "Just because you're Lazarus Stephens's beautiful daughter." Gingerly, his lips closed over the rosy tip of her breast. The denial that had been forming on her lips was never spoken. She could think of nothing other than letting him touch her, assuaging the bittersweet ache that was beginning to throb within her.

His tongue teased her gently and she moaned for more of the savage pleasure. Her fingers twined in his hair, forcing him closer. He took more of her into the warm cavern of his mouth. One hand splayed against her naked back, while the other softly kneaded her breast as he suckled and drew out the sweetness she offered.

Slowly, his lips moved from the naked breast to the delicious mound covered in soft apricot fabric. The nipple was taut and straining against the dress and Trevor placed his mouth over the covered tip, suckling and wetting the fabric with his mouth.

Ashley's head was spinning crazily and she knew that if she didn't stop his masterful lovemaking now, she wouldn't be able to break the magical spell of love he was weaving.

"Touch me," he whispered as he lifted his head and wound his fingers in the ebony silk of her tangled hair and tugged on it, forcing her head backward so that he could nuzzle her exposed throat. Gently he guided her hand to the evidence of his desire.

Ashley let her fingers linger slightly on his straining jeans. The low moan from the back of his throat convinced her that he wanted her as much as she wanted him.

"Oh, God," she whispered. Slowly, she withdrew her hand. "I...I can't." Tears of frustration stung her eyes.

"Shhh...Ashley," he said. He kissed her eyelids and tasted the salt of her tears. "Just let me love you."

"I don't know you, Trevor," she said, trying desperately to rise above the lustful urges of her body. Never before had she been so tempted by a man, so ravaged by desire. Never had the ache within her throbbed for a release only he could offer.

"You will," he promised, gently rising on one elbow. His eyes took in the tangled disarray of her blue-black hair, the mystic allure of her green eyes and the swelling invitation of her firm breasts. "I've waited a long time for you," he vowed, as one long finger traced the column of her throat, past the hill of her naked breast, to probe beneath the apricot dress draped over her waist. "I can wait a few more days."

"And what makes you think that I'll agree?"

He smiled despite the strangling ache in his loins. "Because you want me as badly as I want you."

"You're so damned sure of yourself, aren't you?" she asked, her breath still ragged.

"When I have to be." His finger traced the definition of her lowest rib. "You and I have so much in common, you see."

"So you think it's fate. Right?"

"Most definitely not."

"What then?"

His eyes drove into hers as if he were searching for the darkest part of her soul. "It's a case of a man being obsessed with a woman."

She laughed at the absurdity of the situation, holding the bodice of her dress over her breast. "Obsession? You can't be serious!"

His eyes darkened dangerously. "Just wait and see how serious I am." With that, he hoisted himself from the floor and offered a hand to Ashley, who accepted his help.

When she straightened and managed to slip her shoulder strap back into place, he took hold of her arms and roughly pulled her against him. His lips moved suggestively over hers. "I'll see you tomorrow."

Her breath caught in her throat. "I have plans," she offered lamely.

"Cancel them." With his final words, he left her and walked out of the door.

"Bastard," she muttered under her breath, determined never to see him again.

Ashley spent a sleepless night dreaming of making wild and wanton love to Trevor and in the morning she admonished herself for her immature lust. She told herself that some of the fascination she felt was because he was the adversary—the one thing in life she had to deny herself.

"He'll use you," she warned herself whenever she caught herself thinking about him that morning, but she couldn't help but look out the window in anticipation whenever she heard a vehicle rumble down the lane.

At ten o'clock there was a knock on the door. Ashley's heart was racing when she answered it and discovered Trevor, his cynical smile in place, standing on the small porch.

"I thought you were going to be busy today," he mocked. His blue eyes twinkled devilishly as they raked possessively over her body.

The anger she wanted to feel refused to surface. "It wasn't anything important." She moved out of the doorway, allowing him to enter. "I thought you might like to go on a picnic."

"That's not exactly what I had in mind—"

"I'll bet not. But I've already saddled the horses and thrown together a lunch," she replied, trying to overlook the hint of seduction in his intense gaze. "It'll be fun."

"Promise?"

"Guaranteed."

He smiled before laughing out loud. "You're full of surprises, aren't you?" he asked with a pleased expression softening his face. "The daughter of Lazarus Stephens saddling horses and making sandwiches—it just doesn't fit."

"Maybe what doesn't fit is your stereotype of spoiled little rich girls who refuse to get their hands dirty."

"Maybe." He shrugged his shoulders and followed her into the kitchen. Ashley pulled a bottle of wine out of the refrigerator and shoved it into the already bulging leather bag, which was slung over the back of one of the kitchen chairs.

Trevor watched her pack. "Saddlebags?"

"How else are we going to carry all this food? What did you expect? A picnic basket?"

"I suppose."

Ashley smiled to herself. "Then I guess my first impression of you was wrong."

"Oh?"

"You're not a cowboy?"

"Far from it." Trevor chuckled to himself at the thought. "I'm working at a law firm in Bend for the summer."

"A lawyer?"

"Not yet. But soon, I hope."

"You're still in school?"

"Willamette University," he replied, taking the bulging leather pouch and slinging it over his shoulder. "I hope to take the bar exam in January."

"And what then, counselor?" she teased, her green eyes dancing merrily. Strange as it seemed, she hadn't felt this happy in years. She was comfortable with this man; the fact that he was her father's rival's son added just a little bit of daring to the relationship.

He hesitated for a moment, sizing her up, and decided there was no reason to hide the truth. "Politics."

There was something in the way he said the word that gave Ashley pause. "Whatever for?"

He grinned cryptically. "To change things, of course."
He held the back door for her and then waited somewhat impatiently while she locked it.

They walked together down the short path that led to
the stables. Diablo and Gustave were tied to the fence and
nickered softly when Ashley approached.

"Looks like rain," Trevor remarked, eyeing the cloudy
sky.

"You're not going to weasel out of this," Ashley
stated. "I worked all morning planning this thing, and
we're going on a picnic come hell or high water."

"Whatever you say, ma'am," he drawled with a bad
western affectation.

"You do know how to ride?"

Trevor positioned the saddlebag on Diablo's broad,
black back. "A little." Diablo stamped a dark hoof and
tossed his head, jingling the bridle in contempt.

"It's all right." Ashley soothed the agitated horse with
a soft pat on the neck before taking the reins of the
smaller horse and swinging into the saddle.

They rode together in silence, Ashley leading the way
on Gustave, a fiery bay quarter horse who had the bad
habit of shying away from any noise. "Don't be such a
scaredy-cat," Ashley admonished as she rubbed Gustave's thick neck.

The dusty path led uphill through sagebrush and pine
trees. After traveling for three miles, they reached the
spot Ashley remembered from her childhood. It was a
barren ridge with an enthralling view of the snow-covered Cascades.

When she stopped, Trevor pulled up next to her and cast an approving eye at the view. "Worth the ride," he muttered as he studied the mountainous horizon. The blue sky had filled with gray clouds that gathered around the highest peaks. "Could be in for some rain," he reminded her.

"Then we'd better eat now," Ashley stated as she swung out of the saddle. "I'm starved."

While Ashley spread a blanket and arranged the food, Trevor tethered the horses. Ashley smiled as she watched him work. "Not bad for a tenderfoot," she teased.

Trevor smiled and took a seat next to her on the blanket.

The first drops of rain started to fall just as Ashley poured the wine. As quickly as possible, they drank the wine and feasted on cold chicken, cheese, grapes and French bread. Even with the threat of rain, the meal was perfect. Ashley, as she laughed at Trevor's witticisms, wondered vaguely if she was falling in love.

Because the storm looked as if it would worsen, Trevor repacked the saddlebags and they started back to the cabin much earlier than Ashley had planned. She had envisioned a warm, lazy afternoon with Trevor, learning more about him.

The summer shower began in earnest about halfway back to the cabin and Ashley was forced to urge Gustave into a trot. Once back on familiar soil, the quarter horse sprinted for the barn with Diablo on his tail.

Ashley was breathless by the time they were back in the stables and her long black hair was tangled from the fast ride.

Trevor unsaddled and cooled the horses while Ashley returned to the cabin, started a fire and unpacked the saddlebags. The wind picked up and the sky grew overcast, darkening the interior of the cabin. Rain pelted against the windows.

The fire had just caught and Ashley was sitting on the hearth attempting to brush the knots from her hair, when Trevor came back into the cabin. Raindrops lingered in his dark hair and reflected the warmth of the crackling flames. The interior of the cabin was filled with the scent of burning wood and hot coffee.

"I...I made some coffee," Ashley stated, straightening and setting the brush aside.

Trevor walked across the short distance separating them and his magnetic blue eyes never released hers. Ashley's pulse quickened at the nearness of him. When his cold lips pressed hungrily against hers, she knew that she would never find the strength to deny him again. His strong, muscular body was tense. She could feel his want in his restraint.

His tongue tested and probed and her lips parted willingly for him. She would offer everything to this exciting, mysterious man, hoping that he would care for her...if only a little.

A rush of liquid heat began to build within her, sending pulsating messages throughout her body. She couldn't think or move when his warm, persuasive lips lingered on her neck and nibbled at the sensitive skin near her ear.

"Tell me you want me," he whispered, his demand gentle.

"You know—"

"Say it!"

"I want you," she admitted hoarsely.

"Why?"

"I don't know—"

"Why, damn it!" He gave her shoulders a shake and forced her to look in his eyes. "Tell me it's not just a game with you. That you're interested in more than a quick one-night stand with the son of Robert Daniels."

The words stung, but she bravely returned his gaze. "Oh, Trevor, it's not because you're a Daniels," she whispered. "I know that I want you and not just for the rest of the afternoon."

His relief seemed genuine and the lines of frustration marring his brow relaxed as his lips found hers in a kiss that was as tender as it was urgent.

His fingers slowly unbuttoned her blouse and he paused only to kiss her downy white skin when the fabric began to gap. Her breasts strained against the wet cotton and tingled in swollen anticipation when his tongue probed near the lace edging of her flimsy bra.

"No more excuses," he whispered against the ripeness of her aching nipples.

Ashley swallowed against the dryness settling in her throat. "I only want to be with you," she murmured, sucking in her breath as he unhooked the front clasp of her bra and pushed both it and her blouse over her shoulders to be discarded in a wrinkled heap on the floor.

Then, gently, using his weight, he forced her to the floor and let his hands run in sensual circles over her smooth, white skin. Though the ache in his loins burned uncomfortably, he forced himself to go slowly, to give as much pleasure as he would extract from the voluptuous daughter of Lazarus Stephens.

She was lying next to him, and her damp, black hair fell over the white mounds of her delicious breasts, brushing over the taut, protruding nipples when she moved her head.

Slowly he descended, and when his mouth covered one rosy point, she moaned in pleasure, running her fingers through the thick, damp strands of his hair. Never had she felt such ecstasy and torment. Without considering her actions, she began to unbutton his shirt, forcing it off his shoulders and letting her fingers run over the tight muscles, the mat of curly black hair and the hard male nipples. His breathing became as ragged as her own and Ashley knew that there was no going back. Tonight she would give herself willingly, gloriously to this man. The fiery union of their bodies would be equaled only by the blending of their souls.

When his fingers toyed with the waistband of her jeans she didn't resist. She belonged to Trevor and she felt an overwhelming sense of relief when his strong hands forced the denim fabric to slide easily over her hips, down her legs and past her ankles to find the same fate as her crumpled blouse.

His fingers lingered on her legs and the warmth within her grew. His eyes held hers as he slowly unzipped his jeans and kicked them off. She saw the reflection of the fire in the passion of his gaze. They were naked together, one man and one woman, high in the privacy of the proud Cascades. The smell of coffee and pitchy wood mingled with the scents of rainwater and sweat to blend together in a sensual aroma.

When he came to her, it was the most natural act she had ever experienced. Slowly he lowered his body over hers, positioning himself so that he could read the expression on her face, withholding the urge to take her in a quick eruption of desire.

At first he had planned to bed her quickly and forget her, but he knew now that he was forever lost to her. He wanted Ashley to feel the exquisite pleasure of their mating.

His face was tight, the lines of strain evident when his head lowered and his lips touched hers at the very moment that she felt his desire touch her soul.

"Trevor," she moaned in resplendent agony as he slowly moved within her. "Please...please..." Her words were fuel to the fire of his white-hot desire. The rhythm quickened until, at last, he could hold back no longer. With a rush of unbound passion, he let go, and Ashley felt the shudder of his release as he collapsed upon her. His weight was a welcome burden. She wrapped her arms around his torso and closed her eyes against the tears of joy threatening to overtake her.

Was it love she felt for this man or merely lust?

The affair had run a torrid course through the rest of the summer. Whenever Ashley would get the chance, she would leave the Willamette Valley and meet Trevor in a private tryst of love in the Cascades. After that first moment of triumph and uncertainty, Ashley knew that she loved Trevor Daniels, not because his father was a rival to Stephens Timber Corporation, but because he was the most exciting and wonderful man she had ever met.

It was a glorious summer filled with dreams and promises, laughter and love. For the first time in her life, Ashley learned how to care for someone other than herself. It felt wonderful. She wanted to shout her love for Trevor from the mountaintops.

Somehow—Ashley suspected that Claud was the source—Lazarus found out that she was having an affair with Trevor. Her father was livid.

"How could you do this to me?" he had raged. Seated at the scarred wooden desk in his den, he seemed suddenly old.

"It just happened, Dad," she had tried to explain.

"Just happened! Don't tell me you're that naïve, for God's sake! All that schooling in France—didn't you learn a damned thing! I'll bet Daniels planned this affair all along."

"That's preposterous," Ashley replied indignantly, but a niggling doubt entered her mind. Hadn't Trevor as much as admitted that he had been looking for her, that he had wanted her for years? Was their affair just a way to seek revenge against her father?

"You're so blinded by love that you can't see the truth when it stares you in the face," Lazarus charged, his complexion turning scarlet. His hands raised into the air in a gesture of defeat and supplication for divine intervention. "That son of Robert Daniels is just using you as a weapon against me! He's obviously trying to dig up some dirt on our family and find some way—no matter how obscure—to blame me for his father's disappearance!"

"This has nothing to do with Robert Daniels," Ashley insisted, but she couldn't forget her first heated conversation with Trevor at Sara Lambert's party.

"The hell it doesn't!" Lazarus's fist crashed onto the desk, rattling the drawers.

"Dad, I love him!" Ashley cried.

"Oh, for crying out loud!" Lazarus braced himself against the desk in his office. His eyes slid from Ashley to the view of the Portland city lights before returning, condemningly, to his only child. "Can't you see that he's using you? If that bastard can't find a way to ruin my reputation, he'll settle for you and yours. He knows that by seducing you, he's wounding me." He ran agitated fingers through his thinning hair and his large shoulders slumped in defeat.

Though Ashley's heart went out to him, she couldn't deny the love she felt for Trevor. "You'd better get used to this, Dad," Ashley warned rebelliously, though her faith in Trevor was beginning to waver.

"And why's that?"

"Because I'm going to marry him."

"Out of the question!" Lazarus's watery blue eyes flamed in indignation. "The man isn't even your social equal, for Christ's sake!" He tapped his fingers restlessly on the desk. "If I were you, I wouldn't get my hopes up. Trevor Daniels has no intention of marrying you. To him, you're nothing more than a quick affair. Take my advice and get rid of him. If you want to get married, why not someone with a little class, like Richard Jennings?"

Ashley stormed out of her father's estate, intent on proving him wrong. Trevor was waiting for her at Neskowin on the coast and she was sure, with just the right amount of persuasion, she could coax him into marrying her now, before he finished law school.

She was sadly mistaken.

The weekend at the beach was wonderful and she kept the fight with her father a secret. They spent the days walking on the rain-drenched sand, and during the nights they lay together, sipping imported wine, warming their feet on the bricks of the fireplace and staring out at the black waves crashing furiously in the winter's storm before making incredible love and promising their lives to each other.

It was heavenly and it ended.

When Ashley finally explained that she wanted to get married right away, Trevor was adamant. He wanted to finish law school and establish his career before taking on the added responsibilities of a family.

"Then what am I supposed to do, sit around and wait while you decide whether you want to run for the presidency?" she replied caustically, the pain of his rejection cutting her to the bone.

His features hardened at the mention of his politics. "Of course not—"

"Then you still want me to wait for you."

"Only a few years."

"A few years." It sounded like the end of the world. All of her fears and her father's prophecies were coming true. For the first time in three months, Ashley doubted Trevor's love.

"Look, Ashley," he whispered, gently running his fingers through the silken strands of her hair. "I love you—I'm just asking you to be patient."

"Patience isn't my long suit."

"It's not forever."

"You're sure about that?"

"Of course." His eyes were clear blue and honest. For a moment she was tempted to believe him.

"Then what about the reason you got to know me in the first place—to try to get me to admit that my family was involved in your father's disappearance. The reason you took the time to get to know me at all was just so that you could get some information from me, information to discredit my father."

"That's not the only reason."

Ashley could tell that he was lying through his straight white teeth. The veiled hatred in his eyes at the mention of Lazarus convinced her that the love she thought they had been sharing was all based on a lie.

"I think it's over for us," she stated, tears stinging her eyes.

"Only if you want it to be."

"There's no other way," she murmured, slowly gathering her things and throwing them into her suitcase. Silently, she prayed that he would back down and apologize, that he would beg her to stay. But it didn't happen.

She left the cottage in the middle of the storm, regretting that she had ever laid eyes on Trevor Daniels.

Chapter Eight

The thoughts of the past took their toll on Ashley and she had to remind herself that what had happened didn't matter. She and Trevor had a bargain and she was going to do her damnedest to prove that all of his accusations about her father, Claud and the timber company were unjust. If he had given her nothing else, Trevor had granted her the chance to clear her family's name. For that much, she supposed bitterly, she should be grateful.

She placed her hands on the floor and straightened from the position she had assumed when Trevor had left her. The cabin was cold. She managed to light a fire in the wood stove in the kitchen to give her a little heat as she packed her things and secured the cabin against the winter weather. She worked without really thinking about what she was doing. Her thoughts, still filled with pain, continued to revolve around the past.

Disgusted with herself for being so maudlin, she walked to the window and looked out at the snow-covered ground. Winter birds, dark against the backdrop of white snow, flitted through the pine needles, chirping out lonely cries as they landed on the ground and foraged in the powdery snow.

"You really can't blame Trevor," she whispered to herself as she saw a bird find the seeds she had placed on the deck. Ashley's breath condensed on the window, clouding the clear panes. "You only got what was coming to you."

Most of the agony she had endured was her own fault. If she had just forgotten Trevor, as she had promised herself that stormy night in Neskowin, the following events never would have occurred. But as it was, blinded by fury and disgrace, Ashley had stormed out of the beach cottage and had returned to Portland.

In the following few weeks after the breakup with Trevor, Ashley had resumed working for her father and had secretly hoped that she might be pregnant. She wanted desperately to have Trevor's baby, a lasting memory of the love affair that wasn't quite strong enough to survive. At the time, she had been sure that a child, Trevor's child, was all she needed to heal the pain.

It hadn't happened. Ashley cried bitter tears of anguish when her monthly cycle resumed and all her hopes of bearing Trevor's child were destroyed. Her dreams of the future had been shattered as easily as if they had been delicate sea shells crushed by the tireless anger of the sea.

Ashley had married Richard out of spite. Richard Jennings was the man she had been dating before she met Trevor. Richard worked for Stephens Timber and was the only son of rich, socialite parents. It hadn't taken long for him to propose to the beautiful and headstrong daughter of Lazarus Stephens.

For her part, though at the time she had suspected that she might be deluding herself, Ashley had hoped that another man would replace Trevor. It didn't take her long to realize that she had been wrong.

The marriage had been a mistake for both Richard and herself. Richard had expected a doting wife interested only in supporting him in his engineering career, but Ashley had shown more interest in the timber business than in homemaking.

It wasn't all Richard's fault that the marriage had failed, Ashley decided with a grimace. Though Ashley had hoped to purge herself of Trevor, and though she had tried to be everything Richard wanted, she had failed miserably. Even Lazarus hadn't gotten the satisfaction of the grandchild he had expected from the short-lived union.

A divorce was inevitable. Lazarus Stephens went to his grave an unhappy, selfish man who never had suspected that his daughter was incapable of providing an heir to the Stephens Timber fortune.

Perhaps it didn't matter, Ashley thought as she walked up the stairs to the loft and opened her suitcase. When she and Richard had divorced, she had lost all interest in owning any part of the vast timber empire. If she had learned anything from her brief but passionate affair with Trevor, it was how to be her own person and still care for other people. Trevor had helped her mature. By leaving her, he had forced her to rely on herself and become self-sufficient.

Maybe that was why her marriage had failed; she'd been too strong, while Richard was weak. It hadn't been Richard's obvious affairs that had finally gotten to her; it had been his lack of character and strength.

What's the point of dredging it up all over again? she asked herself as she folded her clothes and placed them in the open suitcase on the bed. The sheets were still rumpled in disturbing evidence of her recent lovemaking with Trevor. She swallowed the urge to cry and hastily straightened the bedclothes.

Working swiftly, she managed to clean the cabin, pack her bags and bundle up all the reports from the Bend office. As she took out the garbage she noticed an empty champagne bottle and remembered how she had shared a glass of the sparkling wine with Trevor in front of the fire the night before. It seemed like weeks ago, when it had only been hours. Could so much have happened in so short a time?

When she finally had packed everything into her Jeep, she returned to make sure the fire was no longer smoldering and to cast one last, searching glance around the interior of the rustic home. Her heart ached painfully. She wondered if Trevor was still at the Lambert cabin just a few minutes away. She pushed the nagging question aside and frowned. She couldn't run to him—not yet. Until she had cleared her father's name, she had nothing to offer Trevor.

"That's life," she muttered to herself, climbing into the Jeep. "Merry Christmas, Ashley," she chided with a self-effacing frown. She turned the key in the ignition and the trustworthy engine sparked to life. Ashley drove away from the snow-covered cabin without once looking back.

It had grown dark by the time Ashley made it back to the Willamette Valley. The blackened skies were moist and the city streets of Portland were slick with rain. Most of the large homes in the West Hills were illuminated with colorful Christmas lights that twinkled in the gathering darkness and were reflected in the raindrops collecting on the Jeep's windshield before the wipers slapped them aside.

Her father's home was a huge, Tudor structure with seven bedrooms and five baths. Why he had ever purchased so large an estate was beyond Ashley, as Lazarus had never remarried and had no children other than herself. Most of the bedrooms had never been occupied. It seemed an incredible waste.

As Ashley turned up the cedar-lined drive, she noticed that the interior lights of the house were glowing warmly.

Ashley smiled to herself, knowing that Mrs. Dever-aux, a fussy French lady who had been Lazarus's housekeeper ever since Enora's death and was still in charge of the house and grounds, must have guessed that Ashley would return tonight.

"Wouldn't you know," Ashley said to herself, pleased that Mrs. Deveraux had thought about her. The kindly old woman still treated her like a child. Tonight it would be appreciated. What Ashley needed right now was a warm meal and a hot bath. Once refreshed, she was sure that she could tackle the mountain of computer print-outs once again.

No one answered her call when she entered. Ashley left her bags at the foot of the grand, oiled-oak staircase and walked into the kitchen, where she found a note from Mrs. Deveraux tacked to the refrigerater door. The message was simple: Mrs. Deveraux had gone out to the movies, would be back around ten and had left a crock of soup in the refrigerater. Also, as a postscript, there was a message from John Ellis, the accountant for Stephens Timber, requesting that Ashley call him the minute she was back in town.

The note made Ashley uneasy. There was no telling what Claud had done after calling Ashley this morning. She couldn't help but wonder if her cousin had pumped John for information after getting no satisfaction from her.

After heating the homemade chowder in the microwave, Ashley dialed John's number at home and let the soup cool.

"Hello?"

"John? This is Ashley."

There was a sigh of relief on the other end of the connection. "Are you back in town?" John's voice sounded anxious, almost fearful.

"Just got in."

"At your father's house?"

"Yes. Why—"

"Good! I'll be there in about half an hour."

"Slow down," Ashley demanded, unnerved by the calm man's uncharacteristic impatience. Her palms were beginning to sweat. There was something about the conversation that made her more than slightly uneasy. "What's going on?"

"I'll talk to you when I get there." With that, he hung up the phone and Ashley was left to consider the unusual conversation.

"What the devil?" she wondered, as she sat down at the kitchen table. Her mind was racing when she tested the soup with the tip of her tongue, decided it was the right temperature and began eating the delicious meal of hot chowder and warm biscuits.

Had John discovered something out of the ordinary in the financial reports? What was it that made him sound so worried and concerned? It was almost as if he were frightened of something...or someone.

"You're beginning to sound as paranoid as Trevor," she admonished herself, smiling slightly at the rugged image her willing mind conjured.

Ashley finished her soup and placed the bowl in the dishwasher just as the doorbell rang. She walked to the front door, opened it and ushered in a very agitated John Ellis.

"What's going on?" she asked as he shed his coat and tossed it carelessly over a bent arm of the wooden hall tree near the door.

"That's what I want to know."

They walked into the formal living room and John stalked from one end of the elegantly furnished room to the other.

"Did you find something suspicious in the books?" Ashley asked, her throat beginning to constrict. Something was wrong—very wrong. John was usually a calm individual known for his attention to detail and sound judgment.

Tonight his face was flushed and his eyes darted nervously from Ashley to the door, the window and back to Ashley again. Several times he rotated his head, as if to relieve the tension in his neck.

"I don't know—" He held his hands, palms up, in her direction. He seemed genuinely confused.

"Take your time," Ashley insisted. "Have a seat and let me get you a cup of coffee, or brandy?"

"Anything." He looked as if he didn't care one way or the other. He was restless and uneasy.

She combined the two drinks and gave him a black cup of coffee laced with brandy. He took the mug, drank a long swallow, and then settled back in one of the stiff chairs near the windows.

Ashley took a seat on the corner of the couch and sipped her coffee. "Okay, so tell me what's happening?"

"I don't know, but I don't like it. Claud is suspicious."

"About the reports I requested to be sent to Bend?" Ashley guessed, knowing the calculating nature of her cousin. It was too bad Claud was so well qualified for his job; his sharp mind and legal background made him indispensable.

"Right. For the last few days he's been questioning me—make that grilling me."

Ashley nodded. Her features showed none of her inner distress. "What'd you tell him?"

John rolled his myopic eyes toward the ceiling. "Nothing, I think. He asked why there were so many printouts and I said that you wanted to go over the books and get a feel for running the company. Claud told me that you could never possibly need that much paper, and I told him that I was just sending you what you requested. He didn't like it much, especially when I said that I would do the same thing, if I had inherited a company the size of Stephens Timber and it had been several years since I'd actually worked in the business."

Ashley let out a long, ragged breath. "Did Claud buy your story?"

Shrugging his shoulders, John shook his head. "Who knows? I told him that I was working on this special audit with you and Claud told me that I was to report directly to him. If there were any discrepancies in the books, he wanted to know about them—pronto."

Ashley frowned and tossed her hair over her shoulder as she rubbed her chin. "Did you—report to him?"

John seemed genuinely disappointed. "Of course not."

"Good." The tension in Ashley's muscles relaxed slightly. "So what did you find?"

"Most everything is pretty cut-and-dried," he replied, smiling at his own unintentional pun.

"Except?"

"Except for a couple of things." John drained his cup, reached for his briefcase and snapped it open. He handed a few crisp sheets of paper to Ashley. They were copies of invoices to the Watkins Mill in Molalla.

Ashley's heart nearly stopped beating when she saw the price Claud had charged for the timber and the date on the invoice. "This...this happened last June?" she asked, her throat constricting. The transaction occurred only a few weeks before the bribery charges were made against Trevor.

"Right. And the price of the timber is way off—ridiculously low. At first I thought it had to be a computer error. We were selling rough timber at three times that much."

"But you changed your mind?" Ashley prodded, barely daring to breathe. Something in John's mannerisms told her to brace herself.

John adjusted his glasses and scowled. "Yes. It just didn't make any sense to me."

"But now it does?" Ashley was almost afraid to ask.

"No. I know how it happened, I just don't understand why."

"What do you mean?"

He seemed to hesitate before he reached into his brief-case and extracted some gray photocopies of invoices, which he handed to Ashley. "I did some more checking. Claud was the one who gave the mill the price break, but he had your father's approval."

Ashley let out a shuddering sigh. "You're sure about that?"

"Got the memo right here." He handed the next incriminating piece of paper to her. Ashley accepted it with trembling fingers.

"Dear Lord," she whispered as she recognized her father's bold scrawl.

"What's this all about?" John asked.

"I'm not really sure," she replied. "But I'm afraid it means trouble—big trouble."

"I thought so." The young accountant rose and paced around the room. "I'm not too crazy about being in the middle of this," John admitted, "whatever the hell it is." He regarded his employer intently. "I thought at first that this might just be a power struggle between you and Claud. But there's more to it than that, isn't there?"

"I think so."

"Does any part of it have to do with Trevor Daniels?" The question sent a cold shock wave through Ashley.

"Why would you think that?"

"I just put two and two together." John's mouth slanted into a sarcastic grin. "That's my job."

"And did you end up getting four?"

"I think so." John held up one finger. "Claud's been furious ever since you took over." Another finger was raised. "You ask me for all of these reports. The only discrepancy concerns the Watkins Mill. Beau Watkins, the owner, was the one who was involved in that bribery mess with Daniels last summer, wasn't he?"

Silently, Ashley nodded.

"Right." He held up a third finger. "Claud's been storming around the office ranting about Daniels's bid for the Senate. It's really a sore spot with him. Therefore—"

"You deduced that Trevor was involved."

"Bingo." The fourth finger straightened.

Ashley couldn't lie. She was asking too much of John to expect him to follow her blindly. "Trevor's convinced that there are shady dealings within the company."

"That's hardly today's news."

"I know." Ashley sighed. "But he thinks that Claud would go to any lengths to ruin his chances in the senatorial race."

"What lengths?" John's expression was grim.

Ashley shrugged indifferently, though the skin was stretched tightly over her cheekbones and her stomach was knotting painfully. "Bribery, sabotage..."

"Attempted murder?"

"He implied as much," Ashley admitted.

John ran unsteady hands over his chin. "I can't believe that Claud would be involved in anything like that."

"Not only Claud, but my father as well."

"No way!" But the pale accountant didn't seem convinced.

"I have to prove that they're innocent."

John looked at the incriminating memo and invoices. "I only hope we can."

"If we can't, then we'll have to face up to the problem, won't we?" Ashley asked the stricken young man.

"Nothing else to do."

"Good. Then we're both of the same opinion." She strode across the room and stared out at the black drizzly night. The city lights of downtown Portland twinkled in the distance. "What I want you to do is request a leave of absence. Use any excuse you want to, maybe a medical reason, too much stress on the job, that sort of thing. Then you can come here and work. You'll be paid just the same, and you can work without Claud staring over your shoulder."

"Just in case we find something incriminating."

"Exactly."

John took in a deep breath before cracking a nervous smile. "All right," he agreed.

Ashley smiled. "You don't have to do this, you know."

"Why not? Because it might get dangerous?"

She sobered. "I don't think so. At least I hope not. If I really thought there were any danger involved, I wouldn't ask you to be a part of this. It's just that there aren't many people I can trust at the company."

"I know. And I like being one of the few."

"I do appreciate it, John."

The accountant smiled. "Then keep it in mind the next time I'm up for a raise."

Ashley laughed. "It's a deal."

John gathered his coat and briefcase and left a few minutes later.

A thousand questions filled Ashley's mind. Was Claud involved in a plan, as Trevor had claimed, to keep him out of the primary in May? And what about the accident and bribery charges? Could Claud or Lazarus have been part of such a deadly scheme?

Ashley picked up her suitcases and began to trudge up the stairs. What about the disappearance of Robert Daniels? All these years Trevor had maintained that Lazarus had been involved in a plot which had led to Robert's... Ashley shuddered. If Robert Daniels wasn't dead, why had he abandoned his family? And where was he now?

"I'm too tired to think about any of this," she told herself as she reached the upper floor, deposited her bags in her room and went into the adjoining bath. She turned on the water to the sunken tub and began removing her clothes.

Could all of the wicked rumors be true? Had she hidden her head in the sand to avoid facing the truth about her father? She stared at her image in the mirror. She was a mature woman today, worldly wise, slightly cynical, and she wasn't afraid to face up to the truth. She only wished that she had been wiser when she was younger and hadn't been so blindly trusting of her father or Trevor.

After peeling off her clothes and pinning her hair loosely on her head, she settled into the hot tub and moaned as the water covered her body. "Dear Lord, what a mess," she whispered to herself. Closing her eyes, she wondered vaguely where Trevor was, and with whom.

Trevor paced between the cedar walls of the Lambert cabin like a caged animal. He alternately stared out the window and glanced at the telephone. The argument with Ashley this morning had been a mistake and all day long he had half expected Ashley to call or drive over seeking amends.

Maybe that was asking too much of her. If he knew anything about that woman it was that she had inherited her father's stubborn pride.

His hands clenched and relaxed at his sides as he swore, walked across the room and picked up the telephone. He dialed the number of Ashley's cabin angrily and waited with impatience as the flat rings indicated that Ashley wasn't there.

"Answer it," he ground out, desperation taking hold of him. All day he had tried to convince himself that what he had overheard this morning had been innocent. If Ashley had wanted to deceive him, she wouldn't have taken the chance to speak with Claud.

But Claud had called her.

"You're making a mountain out of a molehill," he told himself as he replaced the receiver and took a long drink from his warm bourbon.

Then why had she left? It wasn't like Ashley to run away. She'd only done it once before and that was because he had asked her to wait for him. That time she had run to another man and married him. His fingers clenched around the short glass and the cold taste of deception rose in his throat.

He finished his drink and set the empty glass on the table. His lips had tightened over his teeth when he dialed the phone again. This time there was an answer.

"Hello?"

"I'm on my way back to the valley."

"About time," Everett replied. "You missed a couple of Christmas parties that could have been feathers in your cap."

"Give the governor my regrets."

"Already done." There was a slight hesitation in Everett's voice. "Did you accomplish what you set out to?"

Trevor's smile was grim and filled with self-mockery. "No."

The statement should have put Everett's worried mind at ease. It didn't. The campaign manager came directly to the point. "So what are you going to do about Stephens Timber?"

"I'm not sure."

"And Ashley?"

"I wish I knew."

"I hope you come up with some better answers before you start campaigning in earnest, my friend."

"I will."

"Then you didn't find anything out about your accident or the bribery charges?"

"No—not yet."

The reply sounded ominous to Everett. "Then, forget them. At least for now."

"A little difficult to do," Trevor stated, rubbing the bandage over his abdomen with his free hand.

"Concentrate on the election."

"I am."

"Good." Everett let out a relieved sigh.

"You worry too much."

"With you, it's a full-time job. When will you be back?"

Trevor's eyes narrowed as he stared out the window at the darkness. "Tonight."

"Call me when you get in. I'll meet you at the house."

"See you then." Trevor hung up feeling suddenly very old and incredibly tired. He raked his fingers through his coarse hair and sat on the edge of a recliner positioned near the windows. What if Ashley was coming back to the cabin? What if she had only gone out for the day—shopping, or to clear her head. What if she was, now, at this very moment, returning?

"You're a fool," he muttered under his breath, "a damned fool!" Once again he reached for the phone.

Everything was going as planned. John Ellis had requested a three-week medical leave, which Ashley had granted. Claud had muttered unhappily when he heard that the head of the accounting department was taking an unscheduled leave of absence, but hadn't made too big a deal about it.

"Why now?" Claud had grumbled.

"Because he's ill—stomach problems. Probably too much stress on the job," Ashley had answered with a patient smile, though her throat constricted with the lie.

"Lousy timing, if you ask me," Claud had pointed out. "Year-end is always a bitch for the accounting department. Ellis couldn't have picked a worse time if he'd tried."

"Give the man a break, for crying out loud. He'll be back soon. I'm sure that the rest of the staff is perfectly capable of pulling his weight, at least for a couple of weeks."

Claud had glared unhappily at Ashley for a few uncomfortable minutes. Then, with a sound of disgust, he had snapped open the morning edition of his favorite financial journal and turned his attention back to an article dealing with mining rights.

Ashley, displaying professional aplomb despite the fact that her knees were shaking, turned on an elevated heel and walked briskly out of Claud's office. Deception had always been difficult for her, even with her slightly underhanded cousin. It had been difficult hiding the fact that John Ellis was working at her house in the West Hills. So far, no one knew that he was there other than Ashley, John's wife and Mrs. Deveraux, who were all sworn to secrecy.

This cloak-and-dagger business will be my undoing, she thought ruefully as she entered her own suite of offices. *I'm just not cut out to be a spy.*

She sat down wearily in the chair her father had occupied for so many years, closed her eyes and rubbed her forehead. The nagging headache behind her eyelids began to throb.

In the last week, neither she nor John had found any other incriminating evidence against either Claud or Lazarus. Even if her father had been involved with Beau Watkins of the Watkins Lumber Mill in Molalla, that didn't necessarily mean that he instigated the bribery charges. So far, the evidence was only circumstantial at best.

But the invoices represented the first set of concrete facts indicating that Trevor's charges against her family might be more than the idle speculation of a wronged son.

Thoughts of Trevor, his eyes narrowed suspiciously and his chin set in ruthless determination, invaded her mind. His charges against her father and Claud couldn't be ignored. What about the spraying of the pesticide near Springfield? Did Lazarus understand the health hazards involved and then just go ahead with the spraying, neglecting the welfare of the public? Ashley couldn't find it in her heart to believe that her father would do anything so cruel. Though not a particularly warm individual, her father had taken care of her when Enora, Ashley's mother, had died.

Ashley didn't hear Claud open the door. She was so wrapped up in her own morbid thoughts that Claud had advanced upon the desk before she realized he was in the room.

He slapped a magazine down on the polished walnut desk. The glossy periodical was open to the current events section. Accompanying a short article on politics in Oregon was a snapshot of Trevor. Ashley's heart nearly skipped a beat as she looked at Trevor's intense expression and the glitter of determination in his eyes. The bold letters of the headline were a question: TREVOR DANIELS, OREGON'S NEXT SENATOR?

"We've got to stop this before it turns into popular opinion," Claud stated. One of his short fingers poked at the snapshot of Trevor.

"Stop what?"

"Daniels, for God's sake." Claud dropped into a chair near the desk. His dark eyes were clouded in disgust. "Read the article. The reporter acts as if Daniels is a shoo-in in the primary!"

"The latest polls show that—"

"The hell with the polls. It's the election that counts."

"And you're afraid that Trevor will win."

Claud let out an angry gust of air. "Damn right. If he does, we may as well close down."

Ashley's arched brows pulled together as she studied her cousin. Her heart was pounding warily in her chest. "Why?"

"He's out to crucify us."

"By us, do you mean you and me, or the company?"

"Same thing."

Ashley gathered her courage and met her cousin's furious glare. "Why does Trevor Daniels threaten you?"

Claud looked at her as if she were insane. "You still don't understand, do you?"

"Understand what?"

"The man's sworn that he'll get us one way or the other. He still blames your father and the timber company for the fact that his old man ran off with another woman—or whatever. Not only that, he thinks that someone here was involved in the bribery charges leveled against him last summer."

Ashley held her breath, watching, waiting, while Claud confided in her. Claud paused, rose from the chair and, after ramming his hands into his pockets, walked over to the window.

"Were we?" she asked softly.

Claud braced himself on the window ledge and smiled cynically. "Of course not, Ash! What would be the point?"

"To discredit a political adversary—"

"Bah!"

"You just stated that we had to do something about him."

"We do." Claud's fingers drummed nervously on the windowsill. "But something legal."

"Such as?" Ashley held her chin in her hand and her wide sea-green eyes noted all of Claud's aggravated movements.

"Back the other candidate."

"Orson?"

"Right. Bill Orson is Trevor's biggest competition in the primary. He was also pretty tight with your dad. He's the logical choice." Claud frowned thoughtfully.

"I'm not sure—"

"Look, Ashley, we're running out of time. Daniels is beginning to get a lot of press." He pointed a condemning finger toward the magazine. "National publicity. We've got to do what we can to protect our interests."

"Don't you think you're jumping off the deep end?" Ashley asked. "We're only talking about the primary and it's still several months away. Even if Trevor wins in May, he'll still face the other party's candidate in November."

"If he gets the chance."

"Which you want to thwart."

Claud pulled at the edge of his mustache. "That's putting it a little bluntly, but sure, let's call a spade a spade. If Daniels somehow managed to get himself elected, it would be a disaster!"

"His own family is in the logging business," Ashley replied. "Don't you think you're overreacting?"

A cruel smile touched Claud's thin lips. "What I think is that you're still carrying a torch for that bastard! God, Ashley, when will you ever grow up? He used you!"

Ashley crossed her arms over her chest. "And I think you're boxing with shadows."

Claud laughed out loud. "You still think you have a chance with him, don't you?" Ashley had to bite back the hot retort forming on her tongue. Angering Claud any further wouldn't accomplish anything. "Well, I'm inclined to agree. I wouldn't be a bit surprised if Trevor came sniffing around you, at least until after the election. That way he could stop the opposition before it began. All the easier for him.''

Ashley swallowed back her indignation. ''If you think you can get me to go along with whatever it is you want by insulting me, Claud, you're wrong.''

Claud shrugged his bulky shoulders. ''I wouldn't want to do that, cousin dear. After all, you're my boss.''

''And that still sticks in your craw.''

''A little.'' Claud frowned to himself. ''But what concerns me more is the upcoming primary. You may as well reconcile yourself to the fact that we've got to do all we can to stop Daniels before all hell breaks loose.''

With his final words, Claud walked past the desk, took one last look at the magazine article and left the office.

''You're wrong,'' Ashley whispered as the door closed behind her cousin, but his accusations had hit their mark. Had Trevor pretended interest in her just to get what he wanted from her?

The long nights of lovemaking came to her mind and Ashley remembered the honesty in Trevor's clear blue eyes. ''If anyone's being deceptive,'' she thought aloud, ''I'm willing to bet it's you, dear cousin,'' she mimicked. ''And I'm not about to back a bastard like Bill Orson!''

Finding new resolve, she reached for the phone, intent on calling John Ellis. The sooner she found answers to Trevor's questions, the better.

Chapter Nine

That's it," John announced, his weary voice filled with relief.

"You're sure?" Ashley couldn't believe that the task that had seemed so monumental a few weeks ago was now finished.

"There's nothing else." John's expression was one of certainty. Other than the incriminating invoices and memo from Lazarus, John had found nothing to substantiate Trevor's accusations against Stephens Timber.

Ashley should have been jubilant, but she wasn't. "You've checked through everything?" Her fingers tapped nervously against her chin as she sat in the chair facing the desk. John was sitting behind mounds of computer printouts, each carefully labeled and banded together on the top of Lazarus's desk in the den of the stately old manor.

"I've gone over every piece of paper you've brought me." John leaned back in the chair and propped his boots on the desk in a gesture of satisfaction. He stretched and even from where she was sitting, Ashley could hear his vertebrae crack. How many hours had the poor accountant sat at her father's desk, poring over black-and-white figures?

Ashley tried to accept John's audit as final, but during the last couple of weeks with Claud at the office, she had begun to doubt her earlier convictions about her family's innocence. Working with Claud on a daily basis had forced her to face up to the fact that the man had no sense of moral responsibility. Dollars and cents were his only motivation.

Abruptly she got out of her chair and paced anxiously between the desk and the window. The city lights of Portland winked seductively in the clear, black night.

"I thought you would be relieved," John remarked.

"I am—sort of."

"But?"

"These reports are all recent—all in the last six months."

"What're you getting at?"

She stopped near the window and stared at the cloudless night. "I want to clear the family name once and for all. There are a couple of things I want to check out, but it will have to be done at the office. If I take home the reports I need, Claud will become suspicious."

"Why?"

"Because they're old. Some of the documents won't even be on the computer," she thought aloud, her eyes piercing the blackness of the still night.

"What will you be looking for?"

Ashley smiled cryptically and faced him. "I don't know. I won't until I see it. But I want to check the records about the time of the Springfield spraying." She saw the look of protest in the accountant's eyes and she continued. "I want to see the books from day one—when Dad started the company—"

"Because of Robert Daniels's disappearance?"

Ashley let out a long sigh. "Right."

"I don't think you'll find anything," John offered, hoping to give some comfort to her worried mind.

"Let's just pray that you're right."

Later, after John had left for home, Ashley sat in her father's desk chair, worrying about the future. Several times she considered calling Trevor and once she had even gone so far as to reach for the phone. But she hadn't. Her pride forbade it. She sighed and let her hand fall to her side.

Ashley felt that she couldn't go to Trevor until she was certain of all the facts. The small piece of evidence against Claud and Lazarus would only add fuel to Trevor's inquisitive nature and Ashley wanted to be prepared with all the answers to his accusations before she saw him again.

If she saw him again. The argument between them was still unresolved and Ashley doubted if there would ever be a time when they could feel the freedom and love they had shared while alone in the mountains. *It was all just a lie*, she tried to convince herself, but the memory of Trevor's intense blue eyes, filled with honesty and raw passion, still touched a very vital part of her. She found herself hoping that he still cared, if only a little.

For the last two weeks, each time she had picked up a newspaper, Trevor's face had been plastered all over it. Claud was no longer worried about Trevor's bid for the Senate, he was downright furious that the polls showed Trevor Daniels leading the race.

Just the previous week Ashley had walked into Claud's office and overheard the tail end of a telephone conversation.

"I don't care what we have to do," Claud had stated emphatically, his lips white with rage, just as Ashley had walked into the room, "we can't let that son of a bitch win!"

Ashley had known instinctively that Claud was referring to Trevor, but she pretended that she hadn't understood the conversation.

Claud had glanced in her direction, paled slightly and then changed the course of the discussion, as if he were talking to an advertising executive about a future ad campaign.

Ashley's step faltered sightly and her heart filled with dread, but she didn't call Claud on the lie, knowing that it would be better for everyone concerned if Claud didn't think she was suspicious of him.

At that point, she had become convinced that Trevor's accusations about her family weren't completely idle speculation on his part. The look of pure hatred and ruthlessness that had crossed Claud's face while he was on the phone had been blood-chilling.

Just a few more weeks, she had thought to herself. *Just until John and I have all the evidence available. Then, when I know what really happened in the past, I'll confront Claud and give him his walking papers.* No matter how valuable he was to the timber company, Ashley knew that Claud was power-hungry and dangerous. Just like her father.

In the days that followed, John had returned to the office and when Claud would go out for an afternoon, John and Ashley would go over the old records of the timber company. There never seemed to be enough time to sort through all the handwritten documents, but at least Ashley felt certain that Claud wasn't suspicious, not yet anyway.

Ashley's industrious work at the office seemed to convince Claud that she was interested only in the timber company. If he had any earlier thoughts about her relationship with Trevor, he didn't voice them.

Even though she ached to see Trevor, she had made a point of avoiding him for two reasons. The first was that she couldn't face him without being certain of the facts. The argument with him still cut her to the bone and she knew that she could never confront him until she had

uncovered all of the truth and had solid facts to present
to him.

The other reason was Claud. If anyone saw Ashley
with Trevor, or overheard a telephone conversation between them and reported it to Claud, the results would be
disastrous. For, as each day passed, Ashley was beginning to believe that Claud might have been involved in
the planning of Trevor's accident. But she didn't have any
proof. Not yet. She was working on gut instinct alone and
that wouldn't hold up in court, which was exactly where
she supposed her snaky cousin would wind up facing
criminal charges.

Claud had business in Seattle. For the first time since
Ashley had returned from the mountain cabin and her
tryst with Trevor, Claud had been called out of town.
Ashley, as president of the timber company, insisted that
he go; the matter in Seattle was pressing and Claud's legal expertise was desperately needed. Or at least she
managed to convince Claud that his business acumen was
without compare. Though his ego was stroked, he
boarded the plane to Seattle reluctantly, casting Ashley
a final glance that made her shiver with inward dread.

Once back in the office, she forgot Claud's cruel, cau-
tionary stare. For the first time in several weeks, Ashley
felt free. There were things she had to accomplish, one of
which was to contact Trevor. Her heart raced at the
thought and she wondered what kind of a reception she
would receive.

He didn't answer when she tried contacting him at home, and when she called his campaign headquarters an efficient but cold voice told her that Mr. Daniels would get back to her. Ashley waited impatiently all afternoon, busying herself in the office, studying the old ledgers for the company, but Trevor didn't return her call.

At seven o'clock, she went home, helpless to shake the uneasiness beginning to settle on her shoulders. She told herself that he was busy, and for him not to call her wasn't out of the ordinary. Maybe he wanted to wait until he was sure that she was alone. Perhaps he would call tonight.

Frustrated from waiting, Ashley changed her clothes and tried, once again, to reach Trevor at home. There was still no answer and her nerves were frayed as she tried the campaign headquarters. The phone was answered by a recording machine, which played a message about the hours of business.

Ashley slammed the receiver back into the cradle and stalked downstairs. Was Trevor purposely avoiding her? It wasn't unlikely considering the circumstances, except that he had been so damned interested in the records of the timber company. Maybe that was because his accident had been so recent, and now, nearly six weeks later, his attention was focused on the future rather than the past.

A past which included Ashley, and a future which couldn't.

As outspoken as he had been against the Stephens Timber Corporation, Trevor couldn't risk a clandestine relationship with Ashley even if he wanted to, which Ashley seriously doubted.

"Hard day at the office?" Mrs. Deveraux asked when Ashley finally went downstairs and into the kitchen. The housekeeper had prepared Ashley her favorite dinner of pot roast and potatoes. The table was set for one.

"A little rough," Ashley admitted.

The lady with the perfectly coiled white hair pursed her thin lips together thoughtfully as she placed the steaming serving bowls onto the table. "You don't have to go around killing yourself, you know."

"Pardon me?" Ashley was taken aback. Mrs. Deveraux had never made personal comments to her, not since she had moved out of the house at eighteen.

"Just because your father left you the company, doesn't mean that you have to run it."

"But I enjoy it —"

"Bah! It doesn't take a genius to see that you're miserable. How much weight have you lost since you moved back here?"

"Only about five pounds." Ashley set a platter of beef onto the table.

"And on my cooking!"

"I haven't been particularly hungry," Ashley said with a shrug.

"Why?"

"I don't know, no appetite, I guess."

"Hmph! It's the timber company," Mrs. Deveraux pointed out. "It killed your father and it's doing the same with you. Either that, or you're pining for some man you left back at the college."

Ashley felt an uncomfortable lump form in her throat. Because Mrs. Deveraux was the only mother Ashley had known since she was in her early teens, the kindly old woman had a way of making Ashley feel like a contrite child. "I wasn't seeing anyone there."

"Well, sit...sit." Francine pointed a plump finger toward the table.

"You're not eating?"

A twinkle lighted the elderly woman's blue eyes. "Not tonight. I'm going out."

"With George again?" Ashley accused and clucked her tongue. "Another hot date? My, my, this is getting serious."

Mrs. Deveraux chuckled but the smile curving her lips at the mention of her beau quickly faded. "You should be the one going out. You're young and single."

"Divorced."

"Makes no difference. So am I."

Ashley forced a grin she didn't feel. "When I find the right man—"

"Well, you certainly won't find him here." The doorbell chimed and Francine Deveraux smiled. "You're too young and pretty to be losing weight over that damned company. Sell it to your cousin, he would like to own it. Then you'll be a wealthy lady without all these worries."

"And afterward what would I do?"

"Marry a duke, an earl...."

A senator, Ashley thought wistfully to herself.

The doorbell chimed again.

"I must go. You think about what I've said."

"I will. And you have a wonderful time."

"Okay. End of lecture." Mrs. Deveraux kissed Ashley lightly on the cheek and hurried out of the kitchen. As Ashley pierced a piece of the roast with her fork, she heard the door open and the sound of laughter as Mrs. Deveraux greeted George. Within a minute, the door was closed and the great house seemed incredibly empty.

"If only everything were so simple," she said to herself, forcing the delicious food down her throat. Try as she would, she couldn't eat half of what Mrs. Deveraux had served.

With a groan, she got up from the table and tossed the remains of her dinner down the garbage disposal. "What a waste," she muttered before cleaning the dishes and trudging upstairs.

After a leisurely bath, she settled into bed and turned on the television for background noise as she sifted through the pages of a glossy magazine. When the local news came on, Ashley set the magazine aside and turned her attention to the smartly dressed anchorwoman who smiled into the camera.

"Rumor has it that one of the candidates for the senatorial seat vacated by Senator Higgins may be out of the race," the dark-haired woman stated evenly. Every muscle in Ashley's body tensed. "Trevor Daniels, a popular, pro-environmentalist candidate and lawyer originally from the Springfield area who later practiced law in

Portland, will neither confirm nor deny the rumor that he is considering dropping out of the race.''

"No!" Ashley screamed, bolting upright in the bed.

"Mr. Daniels was leading in the most current polls," the anchorwoman was stating, "and so his alleged withdrawal from the race before the May primary comes as somewhat of a shock to the community and the state."

Footage of Trevor, taken very recently at a campaign rally at Oregon State University, showed him talking with the students in the quad under threatening skies. The would-be senator was smiling broadly and shaking hands, looking for the life of him as if he were born to be a politician. Trevor's chestnut hair ruffled in the breeze and his face was robust-looking and healthy.

Ashley's heart contracted at the sight of him, and she noticed more than she was supposed to see. There was something different about him; a foreign wariness in his eyes, and a slight droop to the broad shoulders supporting the casual tweed jacket. Tanned skin stretched tautly across his high cheekbones and the set of his thrusting jaw somehow lacked conviction. What Ashley noticed were the slightest nuances, which had apparently eluded the press.

"Dear God, what happened?" she whispered while the anchorwoman listed Trevor's accomplishments and the pitfalls of his campaign.

"...not only was Mr. Daniels able to fend off false charges of bribery, which occurred last summer, but just recently he sustained an injury in a single-car accident that nearly took his life...." The anchorwoman continued, giving a little background on Trevor's life, including the fact that his father had disappeared ten years ago and though his brother, Jeremy, ran the family business of Daniels Logging Company, Trevor had been known for his tough stands on fair timber-cutting practices and wilderness preservation.

"Again," the woman was saying, "we can neither confirm nor deny this rumor, but if anything further develops on the story, we'll report it to you later in the program. Mr. Daniels is scheduled to speak at a rally in Pioneer Square tomorrow at noon. Perhaps we'll all know more at that time."

When the news turned away from the May primary, Ashley snapped off the set and fell back against the pillows while uttering a tremulous sigh. *Why would Trevor be planning to drop out of the race?* All of his life he had had political aspirations, and he was currently leading Bill Orson in the polls for the primary. Pulling out now just didn't make a lot of sense.

Just then Claud's words of a few days earlier rang in her ears. "We can't let that son of a bitch win!" he had stated to an unknown caller. Could Claud be somehow responsible for the rumor? And was it even true? KPSC wasn't a station to report sensational rumors just to gain viewer attention. Most of the stories reported by the Portland station were purely factual, very seldom conjecture. And yet, the rumor was unconfirmed.

Though it was nearly eleven, Ashley reached for the bedside phone and with quaking fingers punched out the number of Trevor's home. There was still no answer in the grand house on the Willamette, and Ashley wondered if Trevor had moved. He'd never felt completely comfortable in his father's stately home. The vestiges of wealth were too harsh a reminder of the price his father had paid to make Daniels Logging Company successful.

With a sigh, Ashley hung up the phone and settled into the pillows, hoping for sleep. If nothing else, she would be at Pioneer Square the next afternoon to see Trevor, if only from a distance. It seemed like years since she had set eyes on him.

Fortunately Claud was still out of town, so there would be no one looking over her shoulder. *Tomorrow*, she promised herself, come hell or high water, she would find Trevor. Maybe, just maybe, she would force a confrontation with him.

Pioneer Square was a mass of cold, disenchanted citizens. People from all walks of life milled around the red brick amphitheater with frowns. Elderly couples rubbed their hands together for warmth as they stood next to men and women dressed smartly for work in the business offices flanking the city block designated for the square. Gaudily costumed young people with punk hairdos and glittery clothes were joined by a disenchanted group of street people. Joggers paused on their daily run through the city streets on the way to Waterfront Park and young mothers pushing strollers braved the cold February air to hear Trevor Daniels speak.

Ashley stood on the edge of the crowd, her stomach tied in knots. Pieces of angry conversation filtered to her ears.

"You really don't think he'll show?" a jeans-clad student with a scruffy beard asked his friend.

"Nah—politicians, they're all alike—say one thing and do another."

"This guy—he's supposed to be different."

"Sure, he is. Then why isn't he here?"

"Beats me."

"They're all alike, I tell you. They just want you to think that they're something special." The shorter of the two paused to cup his fingers around the end of a cigarette before lighting it. He blew out an angry stream of smoke as he shook his blond head. "I'll tell ya one thing, I'm not votin' for this clown, Daniels. Hell, he can't even show up for his own goddamn rally."

"Maybe his plane was delayed—"

"His plane? Gimme a break. He's supposed to be in town."

"Okay, okay, so the guy's a jerk. Who're you gonna vote for? Orson? That son of a bitch would sell his own mother's soul if there was a dime in it."

"God damn!" The short man ground out his cigarette and frowned. "I was hoping this guy would do something—"

"Meaningful?"

"Give me a break!" His gruff laughter drifted off as the two young men walked toward the podium.

Ashley's anxious eyes skimmed the crowd. Nowhere was there any trace of Trevor. The rally was supposed to begin at twelve and it was nearly twelve-fifteen. Worried lines creased Ashley's forehead as she blew on her cold hands. It was cold, but fortunately dry, and the wind blowing down the Columbia Gorge cut through her coat and chilled her bones.

"Come on, Trevor," she whispered, and her breath misted in the clear air. "If you want to lose this election, you're certainly going about it the right way."

Finally there was a flurry of activity near the podium. Ashley's anxious eyes were riveted to the small stage that had been prepared for the event. The crowd murmured gratefully as a small, round man stepped up to the microphone.

It had been many years since Ashley had seen Everett Woodward, but she recognized Trevor's campaign manager, whose high-pitched voice was echoing in the square. He introduced himself to Trevor's restless public and then politely explained that Trevor had been detained in Salem and that the rally would be rescheduled for another, undisclosed date.

No one was pleased at the news. While some of the would-be Daniels supporters began to disband, a group of hecklers standing near Ashley began to taunt Everett.

"So where is he?" one demanded gruffly. "I don't buy your story that he's in Salem. He was supposed to be here today."

"Yeah, right. And what's all the rumors about him pulling out of the race? What happened? Did he get caught with his hand in the till or something?"

Everett, in his seemingly unflappable manner, ignored the jibes, but his brow was puckered with worry.

The hecklers continued their conversation in private. "If you ask me, Daniels was probably caught with his pants down—in bed with somebody's wife."

"Oh yeah?" The other youth chuckled obscenely and Ashley started to walk away. She was concerned about Trevor, and wasn't interested in any gossip about him.

"Sure, why not? The way I hear it, he was involved with a daughter of some hotshot timber guy—a rival or something—and she was married to someone else."

"Hey, I've got new respect for this guy...tell me about it...."

A protest leaped to Ashley's tongue when she realized the hecklers were discussing her. She had to physically restrain herself from causing a scene and telling the two men that her love affair, that beautiful and fleeting part of her life, had been long over before she married Richard. An unwanted blush flooded her neck and her steps faltered slightly, but she clamped her teeth together, lowered her head against the wind and walked resolutely toward the object of her quest: Trevor's campaign manager.

Everett noticed her approach and a flicker of recognition registered on his placid face. The corners of his mouth twitched downward.

When she was close enough to be heard, Ashley didn't mince words. "I want to talk to Trevor."

Everett smiled coldly. "You and the rest of the voters in this state."

"It's important. I telephoned the campaign headquarters yesterday and a receptionist promised to have Trevor return the call."

"Which he didn't?"

"Right."

Everett was about to make a hasty retort, but changed his mind.

"I don't think he got the message," Ashley informed the round campaign manager.

"Or maybe you didn't. Did it ever cross your mind that maybe Trevor didn't want to talk to you?"

The muscles in Ashley's back stiffened and for a moment she considered letting the subject drop. But too much was at stake. In the past few weeks she had learned that her love for Trevor would never die and that at least some of the pain in the past was her fault for not trusting him. It was imperative that she see Trevor again. With newfound strength she swallowed her pride.

"Which is it?" she demanded, her muscles rigid. She braced herself for the rejection she was sure would follow. "You're his campaign manager, and from what I understand, very good at what you do. Certainly Trevor would confide in you, let you know if he didn't want to see me again."

Everett considered the woman standing before him. The pride and determination in the lift of her chin were compelling. Ashley Stephens Jennings was a far cry from the spoiled timber brat she had once been.

He fingered the handle of his umbrella and his gaze left her to study the architecture of the buildings surrounding the square. "I think it would be best if you forgot about Trevor Daniels," he ventured. "It would be political dynamite if the press found out that you were seeing him again."

"That's ducking the issue, Everett. Has Trevor told you that he doesn't want to see me?"

Everett gazed into the quiet fury of her blue-green eyes. There was a new dignity and spirit in her stare. He found it impossible to lie to her. "Right now, Trevor isn't really sure what he wants," the campaign manager admitted.

"Including his ambitions for the Senate?"

The portly man's eyes glittered dangerously. He knew he'd given too much away to the becoming daughter of Lazarus Stephens. "Leave him alone, Ashley," he warned. "Before Trevor saw you again, he knew what he wanted. And now...oh, hell!" A fleshy fist balled in frustration.

"And now what?" Ashley whispered, her throat constricting.

Everett laughed feebly. "I guess you and your father got what you wanted all along," he said in disgust. "Single-handedly you seem to have convinced the best goddamn man in Oregon to back down from his one shot at making it. Do you know what you've done? Have you any idea what you alone have cost this state?" His face reddened with conviction and his hands gestured helplessly in the air. "He would have been good, Ashley, damned good."

With his angry remark, he turned toward his car, and then cast another warning over his shoulder. "Give up, Ashley, you've gotten what you wanted. It's over for him. Now, for God's sake, leave the poor bastard alone!"

After grinding out his final, gut-wrenching advice, Everett slipped into the dark interior of a waiting cab. The battered car roared to life, melding into the traffic heading east toward the Willamette River.

Ashley was left standing alone in the wintry air. She felt more naked and raw than she had since the last time she had seen Trevor walk out the door of the mountain cabin. Shivering from the frigid wind, she wrapped her arms under her breasts.

An ache, deep and throbbing, cut through her heart and pounded in her pulse. "Dear Lord, Trevor," she whispered, "what happened to us?" She looked up at the cold gray sky and tears gathered in the corners of her eyes. How had she been so blind for so long? Why had she let other people, other things, unnecessary obstacles separate her from him? Was it pride, or was it fear of the truth that had kept her from facing the fact that she loved him more desperately than any sane woman should love a man?

Her fingers were clenched tightly around her abdomen when she heard her name.

"Ms Jennings?"

Unaware that anyone had been watching her, Ashley whirled and faced a young man, no more than twenty-five, who was staring intently at her. His clean features gave no hint of what he wanted.

"Pardon me?" she whispered, carefully disguising the huskiness in her throat with poise.

"You are Ashley Jennings, aren't you—Ashley Stephens Jennings?"

"Yes." She was instantly wary. The last twenty-four hours had been a roller coaster of conflicts and emotions and something in this man's studious gaze warned her to tread carefully.

The young man flashed a triumphant smile. "I thought so. Elwin Douglass." He stretched out his hand and reluctantly Ashley accepted his larger palm in her icy fingers.

"Is there something I can do for you?"

"I hope so. I'm a free-lance reporter." Ashley's heart froze in her throat. "I'm doing a series of articles about the politicians in the primary…and, well, I'm starting with Trevor Daniels."

"Mr. Daniels wasn't here today," Ashley replied, sensing that she didn't want to become embroiled with this young man. "You should be talking to him and I have to get back to work—"

"I'll walk with you. This won't take long," he reassured her. "You're in charge of Stephens Timber, aren't you?" He was writing in a notebook, glancing at her and refusing to be put off.

"Yes. I'm the president. Several people help me handle the management. I couldn't do it alone." Involuntarily she thought of Claud and cold dread stiffened her spine.

A traffic signal on Fifth made her pause. Douglass grabbed the opportunity. "I know. But your company, at least in the past, has been very vocal in condemning environmental candidates such as Daniels."

The signal changed and Ashley stepped off the red-brick curb and onto the wet pavement. "Look, Mr. Douglass. I really don't want to give an impromptu interview right now. Perhaps if you called the office, we could arrange a time that would be convenient for both of us."

The bold reporter refused to take the hint. "Well, there's just a couple of questions."

"Really, I don't think—"

"You're Lazarus Stephens's daughter, right?"

"Of course, but—"

"His only child, the one who got involved with Trevor Daniels several years ago."

"If you'll excuse me," Ashley stated, increasing the length of her stride. The offices of Stephens Timber Corporation were now in view. Ashley was never more glad to see the renovated, turn-of-the-century hotel sitting proudly on Front Avenue.

"Wait a minute. What do you know about this rumor that Daniels is withdrawing from the race?"

That's an easy one, and safe, too, Ashley thought to herself. "Absolutely nothing," she answered honestly. Her smile was well practiced and cool. "Now, seriously, if you'd like to continue this interview, at another time, just give the office a call.'' She fished in her purse, found a business card and extended it to him. ''Right now I have work to do.''

Grudgingly Elwin Douglass accepted the small white card and slipped it into his wallet.

Ashley pushed open the wide glass door of the building and effectively ended the interview. Her chin was held proudly, her strides determined. Despite the warnings from Everett Woodward, and the unspoken insinuations from the reporter, she knew that she had to see Trevor again.

Tonight.

Chapter Ten

Twilight had fallen by the time Ashley arrived at Trevor's stately home. Despite the gathering darkness, Ashley could see that the grand two-story structure hadn't changed much in the past eight years. Built of cedar timbers and bluestone, the English manor stood proudly on the banks of the silvery Willamette River.

Sharp gables angled against the steep roofline, and ancient fir trees guarded the estate. Leaded windows winked in the harsh glare of security lights, which illuminated the rambling structure and cast ghostly shadows over the dormers.

Gathering her purse and her composure, Ashley got out of her car and walked up the rough stone path to the front door. Though she had entered that door dozens of times in the past, her heart began to thud anxiously as she ascended the steps of the stone porch and braced herself for Trevor's inevitable rejection.

Everett's warning echoed dully in her mind—*Leave the poor bastard alone.* What did that mean? It was more than a threat; the campaign manager's words sounded like a plea, as if Everett was attempting to protect Trevor. The thought sent cold desperation racing through Ashley's bloodstream. Why did Trevor need protecting? He had always been a strong, proud man, capable of taking care of himself and finding a way of getting what he wanted in life. He had always stood alone, fighting whatever battles he had to without anyone's help.

Unable to dispel the overwhelming sense of dread settling upon her, she rang the doorbell and waited impatiently. The melodic chimes sounded through the solid wood door, but there was no evidence of life from within the huge house. Fear for the man she loved took a stranglehold on her throat.

The scent of burning wood drifted in the air, indicating that a fire was burning in one of the massive fireplaces within the manor.

She stood alone on the porch and the only sound that interrupted the stillness of the night was her own irregular breathing. Nervously, she stretched upward on the toes of her shoes and peered into the closest window. The room into which she was looking was dark, but there were soft lights glowing in the far doorway, as if illumination from another room was filtering down the corridor. Apparently whoever it was within the manor preferred his privacy.

After a few quiet minutes of indecision, Ashley tossed her hair over her shoulders and rapped sharply on the dark wood door. She had come to see Trevor and she was bound and determined to find him, even if it took her all night. Whoever was in the house would just damned well have to get off his duff and answer the door. After eight years, she was sick and tired of waiting.

Her heart was beating wildly when she heard footsteps approaching the door.

It opened with a moan and she found herself staring into the anxious blue eyes of the man she loved with all her heart. He looked older than she remembered; his hair was unkempt, his eyes dull. *He looks as if he's been to hell and back*, she thought to herself. He was a far cry from the strong, unbeaten man with the flash of determination in his eyes that she remembered so well. Her heart twisted in silent agony for him and the pain he bore.

"Ashley?" Trevor asked, leaning between the door and the frame, as if he were too tired to stand unaided. The scent of Scotch lingered in the air.

His voice was surprisingly indecisive and the thrusting determination of his jaw was undermined by the painful questions clouding his eyes. A stubble of beard darkened his chin and his skin was stretched tightly over gaunt facial features. His clothes consisted of worn jeans and an unbuttoned flannel shirt, which was faded and rumpled, with the sleeves rolled over his elbows as if he hadn't wasted the time or the effort to change in several days.

When he looked into her eyes, the rigid lines near his mouth softened slightly and the tension in his shoulder muscles slackened.

"Ashley...dear God, woman, is it really you?"

She hesitated. Nothing could have prepared her for the tired and broken man she was facing. A faint smile touched the corners of his mouth, but even that seemed an effort. Tears of misunderstanding filled her eyes.

"Oh, Trevor, what's happened to you?" she whispered, her voice catching in the dark night.

"Nothing that matters. At least not now." He closed his eyes as if to push aside the demons playing with his mind. "I've missed you, lady," he admitted roughly, and he opened the door a little wider.

It was all the encouragement she needed. With a strangling sob, she ran to him and wrapped her arms securely around his neck to hold on to him in quiet desperation. All the old barriers that had held them apart for so many years seemed to crumble and fall. His arms held her securely, crushing her body with the power of his, as if he, too, were afraid that she was only a figment of his imagination and would vanish into the night as quickly as she had appeared.

Silvery tears streamed down her face and she drank in the familiar scent of him, all male and warm. There was the lingering trace of Scotch on his breath. When he pressed his lips to hers, she felt as if she would melt into the polished oak floors of the grand entry hall.

"I thought I'd lost you," he rasped, and for the first time Ashley noticed the tears gathering in his eyes. Never before had she seen Trevor cry and there was something endearing in the knowledge that this proud man cared enough to let her see his weakness.

"Shhh...I'm here now. That's all that matters," she murmured, smoothing the disheveled chestnut hair from his eyes and kissing his tear-stained cheeks.

"I won't let you leave me again," he vowed, recovering his composure and kicking the door closed with his foot.

"If I remember correctly, Senator, it was you who left me."

"Not eight years ago, lady. That's when I made my mistake with you. I should never have let you walk out of my life."

"And I shouldn't have walked—"

"Amen."

With a quick movement, he bent and slipped one arm under the crook of her knees, lifting her lithely off her feet.

"What are you doing?" she murmured into his neck as he started to carry her to the back of the house.

"What I should have done a long time ago," he returned. "I'm going to make love to you until you promise that you'll stay with me forever." His words pierced her heart like silver needles, reminding her of a past that held them together only to push them apart. "I've made more than my share of mistakes in my life, but not tonight. I've waited too long for you to show up on my doorstep."

"And what if I hadn't? How long would you have waited?" The warmth of his body seemed to flow into hers, and his rock-hard muscles rippled slightly when he walked. Despite the unspoken questions lingering between them, Ashley felt her body responding to Trevor's captive embrace and the sparks of possession in his eyes.

"I don't know," he replied darkly.

"You could have called."

Shame tightened his jaw. "I was afraid."

"Of me?"

He let out a disgusted sigh. "For you. Whatever it was that I was up against, I didn't want you involved."

"But you asked me to check the company records—"

He placed a silencing finger to her lips. "After our argument, I realized that it had been a mistake to ask you for your help in the first place and then, later..."

"Wait a minute—slow down. What the devil are you talking about?" she asked, her arms still encircling his neck. When she pulled her head away from his shoulder in order to study the anxious lines of his face, she could read nothing but worry in his gaze.

Trevor noticed the confusion in the mysterious sea-green depths of her eyes as he carried her into the den. He shook his head as if to knock out the cobwebs that had gathered in his mind from too many nights without sleep and too many bottles of alcohol to deaden his nerves.

"Not now," he whispered as he placed her on the plushly carpeted floor before the fire. Passion darkened his eyes as he brushed a strand of dark hair from her face and gazed down upon her. His finger traced the length of her jaw, pausing slightly at the pout on her lips. "Tonight you and I are going to forget about all the craziness between our families, all the lies, and all the betrayals. Tonight, we're going to concentrate on each other, just as if the slate were clean."

Her fingers grabbed hold of his wrist, effectively halting the assault on her senses from the sensual touch of his hands. Her words came out in a ragged whisper. "You act as if you expected me to show up here tonight."

His shoulders drooped from an invisible burden and he looked away from the elegant contours of her face to stare into the fire. Drawing his bent legs to his chest, he placed his folded arms over his knees and stared at the scarlet embers of the dying fire. "I didn't think I'd ever see you again," he admitted reluctantly. "I thought you were lost to me forever."

"But why?"

"I almost lost you once before when you married another man."

Ashley felt the burn of her betrayal in her chest. "You know that was a mistake, I told you so. Even Richard would admit it." She touched Trevor gently on his arm, forcing him to turn and face her again. "Don't you know I've never loved another man, not with the passion I've felt with you? I only married Richard because I didn't think you wanted me, and I'll never make that mistake again. It wasn't fair to anyone. Not you, or Richard, or myself. In the past eight years I've learned a lot; one thing is that if you find something you want, I mean really want, you've got to hold on and never let go. I learned that from you, Trevor. That and so much more."

Trevor buried his face in his hands. "I hope you know that I would never do anything to hurt you," he said.

"I do." She didn't question him for a moment. She had come to him and found him raw and naked and vulnerable. For the first time in her life she knew that he cared, that he had always cared as much as he could allow himself.

"And the last thing I would want would be for you to be subjected to any kind of danger."

"Of course—Trevor, why are you talking like this?"

He turned to study her worried expression. Her fingers on his forearm moved slowly, soothingly against his skin. He swallowed against the uncomfortable lump which had formed in his throat and made speech impossible. "I love you," he admitted, his eyes boring into hers.

The movement against his arm stopped abruptly and a sad smile touched the corners of Ashley's mouth. How many years had she waited to hear just those words?

Trevor took her small fingers in his and touched each one to his lips. The moist warmth of his tongue as it slid seductively against her skin forced a tremor of longing to shake her body.

Blue eyes held her fast as his hands pushed her coat off her shoulder before straying to the top button of her blouse.

"I'm not going to let you go," he promised as the first pearl fastener slid through sea-blue silk. "I'm going to keep you here, protect you, and you'll never be able to get away from me again." Another button was soon freed of its bond by the warm insistence of his finger.

Ashley's breathing was rapid, coming in short little gasps, and her heartbeat thundered in her ears. Her breasts rose and fell as his hand slid lower, to the third button. "I've never wanted to get away from you, Trevor," she rasped when her blouse parted and the firelight displayed the French lace of the camisole covering her breasts. His hands touched the silken fabric, and Ashley's fingers wrapped around his wrist to forestall the attack on her senses. There were things she needed to know. Questions that had no answers.

"Why didn't you call or come to me?" She looked up at the strained angles of the face, shadowed now in the fire's glow. There was a weariness about him and the smile he rained on her was bitter, filled with agonized defeat.

"It's better this way. I couldn't take a chance of placing you in danger."

Regardless of the passion smoldering in his midnight-blue gaze, the set of his jaw was grim and rigid. His shirt hung open and as he leaned over her, she noticed that the muscles of his chest were tense and strained. There was no bandage to swath his abdomen, but a jagged red scar sliced across the tanned skin, reminding her of the reason he had sought her out in the lonely mountains.

Lightly, her fingers traced the scar. Trevor sucked in his breath and closed his eyes, as if in pain.

"What's with all this talk about danger?"

He paused a long moment and stared down at the vulnerable and beautiful woman lying on the carpet. Her mysterious eyes were heavy with seduction and the fine lace of her camisole couldn't hide the twin points of her nipples straining against the flimsy cloth. "There's nothing to worry about now," he whispered, lowering his head to the inviting cleft between her breasts. "I'll take care of you...."

She felt the heat of his tongue slide against the lacy fabric as a slumbering desire began to awaken within her. She was lost in her love for this man. Seeing some of his pain and worry only intensified her yearning to be a part of him...and his life.

His fingers twined in the ebony strands of her hair. He whispered words of love against the sensitive shell of her ear before his lips pressed against hers with the fire of too many nights of lonely restraint.

Passion parted her lips and she eagerly accepted the touch of his tongue against hers. Her hands pushed his shirt off his shoulders, lingering over the smooth, hard muscles of his upper arms as the cotton garment slid silently to the floor.

"Make love to me," he murmured when her hands touched his belt and hesitated at the buckle. He rubbed against her, making her achingly aware of the urgency of his desire stretching the faded denim of his jeans.

She moaned in response and slowly removed his pants, letting her fingers slide in a familiar caress down the length of his lean thighs and calves. The corded muscles tensed at her gentle touch, and when her fingers slid against the tender arch of his foot, he began to shake from the restraint he placed upon himself.

Passion glazed his eyes. When at last he was freed of his clothing, he stretched out beside her and gently pushed a satiny strap off her shoulder. The result was that one of her breasts was bared to him. He studied the delicious, ripe mound, before cupping its swollen weight with his palm.

"I love you," he whispered again, lowering his head and taking the taut nipple into his mouth. His tongue circled the straining dark peak, moistening and teasing the ripe bud until Ashley moaned in bittersweet ecstasy.

At last he placed his lips around her breast and began to suckle, drawing out the sweetness within her until she thought she would go mad with desire. She cradled his head in her hands, holding him closer, wishing that she could offer more to him than just her body.

When Trevor finally lifted his head to gaze into her eyes, Ashley's heart felt like a bird trapped in a gilded cage as it fluttered wildly against the prison of her ribs. The shadowed corners of the room seemed distant. All she could see were the bold features of Trevor's face as he slowly lifted her camisole over her head.

After discarding the unwanted garment, his fingers trailed slowly up her stockinged legs.

"Trevor...please," she murmured tremulously before feeling him pulling her skirt and underthings down her hips. Soon she was lying naked with him.

Perspiration dampened his torso and gleamed like oil in the fire glow. He kissed her softly on the lips and rubbed his body against hers, all the while watching for the subtle changes in her expression.

"I want you," she whispered to the unspoken questions in his knowing eyes.

"That's not enough."

She swallowed the hot lump in her throat, understanding the words he yearned to hear. A coaxing hand rubbed against her breast in gentle circles, breaking her concentration and causing the liquid fire within her to pulse through her veins.

She was incapable of thinking of anything but this man lying atop her, teasing her gently by rubbing his rigid length over the soft slopes of her body.

"I love you, Trevor," she said again, her heartbeat echoing in the dark room. "I always have."

A sheen of perspiration covered her body and trickled between her breasts. Slowly, Trevor's head lowered to catch the salty droplet with his tongue. "And I love you, Ashley...." His head lifted and his eyes held hers with all the passion of eight lost years. "I never stopped."

With his traitorous admission, he closed his eyes and gently forced her knees apart, surrendering at last to the fire in his loins and the seduction in Ashley's sea-green eyes. He entered her slowly, but with a determined thrust that claimed her as his own. For too many years he had ached for another man's woman, and in the rush of heat building within him, he attempted to expunge forever the mark of Richard Jennings from Ashley's soul. She was his woman now and forever. If he'd learned anything in the past few weeks it was that nothing else in life was worth a damn.

Trevor's torment was evident in the strain on his face and the unleashed power of his lovemaking. Never had their coupling been more bittersweet than now, and Ashley gave herself to the authority of his touch. The sweet fury within her began to rage, hotter and hotter, demanding release until, at last, she convulsed in a passion born of years of denial.

"Trevor," she cried as she felt his answering shudder, and his weight fell against her. Tears glistened in her eyes and when his breathing slowed, he rolled off her before tenderly cradling her head against his shoulder.

"Nothing will ever come between us again," he vowed, his voice rough with emotion and his breath ruffling her hair.

"How can you be so certain?"

"Because for the first time in weeks, I feel like the master of my own destiny." Softly he kissed the tears from her eyes and fought against his own. "You and I, lady, we're going to get through this and we're going to get through it together."

"If only I could believe—"

"Believe."

She wrapped her arms securely around the man she loved, to drown in the scents mingling in the room—the smell of burning wood, the gentle tang of sweat and the muskiness of stale Scotch.

Tenderly he smoothed her hair away from her face. "I was afraid that you would never come here," he stated, blue eyes regarding her solemnly.

"But I called—"

"And no one answered."

"I left word at the campaign headquarters. The receptionist said you'd call me back."

Trevor stiffened beside her. "When?"

"Yesterday afternoon."

His shoulders relaxed slightly. "I've avoided that place," he admitted, "and I didn't answer the phone when I was here."

"But why?" She touched his shoulder lightly. "What's going on with you? The rumor's out that you're pulling out of the race."

"Is that why you came here tonight?" he demanded, his eyes instantly glittering with smoky blue fire.

"No. But it made me realize I had to see you again...touch you. There are things we need to discuss."

Trevor managed a beguiling smile. "We will, after I fix you something to eat."

"I'm not hungry," she began to protest.

"Come on, indulge me, I'm starving."

"What you're doing is avoiding the issue."

"In the manner of a true politician." He stood up and pulled on his jeans before tossing her clothes to her. "If you want to talk, you'd better get dressed. Otherwise, I won't be liable for what happens." His eyes slid seductively down her body and lingered at the swell of her breasts. "You're too damned beautiful for my own good."

Ashley smiled wryly as she stepped into her skirt and slid the camisole over her head. While adjusting the zipper of the slim skirt, she caught Trevor staring at her. He was leaning against the fireplace and his arms were crossed over his chest as he watched her work with the obstinate zipper.

"A lot of help you are," she muttered.

"If I come over there and touch you, you can bet that I would be pulling down instead of up."

Her head snapped upward. "You were the one who wanted me to get dressed."

"You got it all wrong, lady."

"Don't I always?"

He shook his head and laughed. "You wanted to talk and I told you that would be impossible, unless you had some clothes on. Otherwise, I might get distracted."

"Promises, promises," she teased just as the zipper locked into place.

Trevor's eyes flashed ominously. "I'm not through with you yet, you know. And every time you tease me, I'll extract my own kind of punishment on you later."

"Sure of yourself, aren't you?" Ashley cocked her head to the side and her dark hair framed her face in soft curls.

Trevor shrugged, refusing to be baited by her coy mood, though he wondered to himself how one woman could tear his guts out with a coquettish toss of her head. "With you, I'm never sure of anything."

Ashley sobered instantly. Trevor took her hand and led her to the kitchen near the back of the house.

"I don't think there's much here..." he said, beginning to scrounge through the contents of the refrigerator.

"Doesn't matter. I'm not the one who's starved," she pointed out, staring unabashedly at the way his jeans strained over his buttocks as he leaned into the refrigerator.

"Hmph... Here we go. How about an omelet?"

"Anything—would you like me to cook?"

"Not on your life." Then, when he looked up, he smiled disarmingly. "It might be safer if you did."

Ashley was glad for an excuse to keep busy. While whipping the eggs and grating the cheese, she could feel Trevor's eyes on her and for the first time in weeks she was completely relaxed, as if she had come home from a long and tedious journey.

They ate the meal in silence, and Ashley savored each sweet second she shared with Trevor.

"So tell me," she insisted, clearing the plates from the small table in the windowed alcove just off the kitchen, "what's with all this talk about your withdrawal from the race?"

"So far that's what it is: just talk."

"Where there's smoke, there's fire," she observed.

"You should know all about that."

She felt the muscles of her back stiffen, but when her eyes met his, she knew that the old animosity had mellowed and that Trevor hadn't meant to bring up his accusations against her father.

"That reminds me," she said, wiping her hands on a dish towel near the stove. "I have something for you."

His gaze sharpened. "You found some proof?"

"I wish I knew what it was," she admitted. "It's in my purse...in the den."

Once back in the cozy study, Trevor stoked the fire, while Ashley turned on a table lamp and extracted the documents condemning her father and cousin.

When the fire was blazing to his satisfaction, Trevor dusted his hands on his jeans and approached Ashley. She started to hand him the documents, but Trevor shook his head. "I don't want to know what you found, if it's something that will hurt you or your family."

Ashley's eyes narrowed a fraction. "I don't understand. You asked me, no, demanded is a better word, that I look for evidence against my family. For the last six weeks I've worked my fingers to the bone. Now you don't want it?"

"What I don't want is to hurt you—not anymore. If there is something in those pages—" he pointed to the papers she was clutching "—that would be better off hidden, then I think you should burn them. Right now."

He was offering her a way out, a lifeline for her father's reputation, but she couldn't accept it. If she and Trevor had any chance at happiness, it was by destroying all the myths of the past and laying to rest the lies. Any future they might share would have to be founded on truth.

"Here." She put the papers in his hands. "Let's start over—a clean slate. Remember?"

He took the pages from her trembling fingers and sat on the hearth near the fire. "I'll be damned...."

"It's what you wanted, isn't it? Proof that my father and Claud were behind the bribery charges."

His broad shoulders sagged. "Was there anything else?"

"Not that I could find," she said roughly. "John Ellis and I worked day and night with all the company records. Sure, we could have overlooked something, I suppose, but I doubt it. There was nothing I could find around the date of your accident that would lead me to believe that Claud had any part in it. As for your father's disappearance..." Trevor's eyes sharpened and he watched her face. "...I checked, everything I could think of, as far as ten years back." She shook her head and the firelight caught in her raven-black hair.

"I suppose that may be one mystery that's never solved," Trevor thought aloud. He rubbed the tension from the back of his neck and wondered, for the thousandth time, what had happened to his father. "Now it's my turn to be honest," he stated.

Ashley's heart chilled. Had he been using her? Were all his words of love only to extract what he wanted from her? She couldn't believe it, and yet her heart was filled with dread. "About what?"

"I had a meeting with Claud."

His words settled like lead on the room. "You what?"

"I instigated a private confrontation with Claud—just yesterday. That's why I didn't show up at Pioneer Square. I was in Seattle."

"But Everett said you were in Salem."

"That's where he thought I was. If I had told him that I was flying to Seattle to have it out with Claud Stephens, Everett would have hijacked the plane."

"So what happened?" Ashley asked, almost afraid to hear.

"Claud was his usual friendly self," Trevor replied cynically.

"I'll bet." Claud's words again rang in her ears: *We can't let that son of a bitch win.*

"He wanted, make that insisted, that I pull out of the senatorial race. There had already been some rumors to that effect and Claud wanted to substantiate them."

"But that's ridiculous."

"Precisely what I told your cousin."

"And?"

Trevor rubbed his chin and looked intently at Ashley. "When I refused, Claud got a little nasty. He told me that if I didn't withdraw, he would see to it that not only was my name dragged through the mud, but yours as well. He thought the public would want to be reminded of our past association, and he insinuated that he thought it would make good copy for the local papers, including the *Morning Surveyor.*"

Ashley sagged into a recliner by the window. How far would her cousin go to get what he wanted? Her throat was desert-dry, her knees weak, but her conviction strong. "You can't be bullied by Claud's threats."

"Not as long as I know that you're with me—on my side."

Ashley fought against her tears. "I always have been," she murmured.

He looked as if a terrible weight had been lifted from his shoulders. "Now that you're safe, nothing else matters."

"Except your career."

"Damn my career."

"Trevor, you've worked too long and hard to give up now. It's all within your grasp. Everything you've wanted."

His blue eyes darkened savagely. "What I want, dear lady, is right here."

"Meaning what?"

"You never have understood, have you? I'm asking you to marry me, Ashley, and I'm not about to take no for an answer."

"Are you serious?" Desperately Ashley wanted to believe him, and yet, the entire night seemed like part of a dream.

"I've never been more serious about anything in my life. Will you marry me?" He strode across the room and pulled her out of the chair, forcing her to meet the sincerity of his gaze.

Tears pooled in her eyes and she managed a weak smile. "Of course I'll marry you, Senator. I just wonder why it took eight years for you to come to your senses?"

"Because I've been a fool, Ashley. A goddamned, self-righteous, egotistical fool."

"Join the club."

Trevor laughed aloud before scooping her off her feet and carrying her through the darkened house and up the stairs to his bedroom.

Chapter Eleven

When Ashley awoke the next morning, Trevor was already out of bed. She stretched in the cool sheets and smiled as she remembered making love to Trevor long into the night. They had spent the dark hours passionately entwined in each other's arms, with the only interruption being one telephone call that Trevor had received in the early hours of the morning.

"I thought you weren't taking any calls," Ashley had grumbled groggily when she glanced at the digital display of the clock on the nightstand. The luminous numbers had indicated that it was nearly two in the morning.

"I'm not," had been Trevor's cryptic reply. "Only those that come in on my private line, like this one. Then I know it's important." She felt as if he were holding back something from her but she was too tired to care. After his brief explanation, he had reached for the phone and taken the call, which had been lengthy and very one-sided.

Ashley hadn't been able to decipher Trevor's end of the conversation, and she had been too sleepy to concentrate. Before Trevor had finished talking, she had curled up around him and drifted off to sleep, warm and content as he stroked her hair with one hand while holding the telephone with the other. She had felt the coiled tension in his rigid muscles and had wondered vaguely if there was something seriously the matter, but she had fallen back into a dreamless sleep without any answers to her questions.

This morning the entire incident loomed before her and bothered her a little, but she shoved her worried thoughts aside.

"Your imagination is working overtime again," she chastised herself with a self-mocking smile.

After taking a quick shower, she put her clothes on and brushed her hair before walking down the curved oak staircase to the main floor of the house. The warm morning smells of hot coffee and burning wood greeted her. Ashley was smiling when she breezed into the kitchen looking for Trevor.

The room was empty. There were signs that Trevor had been there; the coffee had finished dripping through the coffeemaker into the clear glass pot, and the morning newspaper had been brought into the house and torn apart. Several sections were still lying haphazardly on the table near the bay window. Ashley scanned the headlines and noticed that the front page of the paper was missing.

It was then she heard the low, angry rumble of Trevor's voice coming from the direction of the den. With quickening steps, Ashley followed the sound. What could have happened? The sketchy memory of the late-night telephone call entered her mind and her heart began to race.

Trevor sounded furious. His rage shook the stately timbers of the old house. "This is the last straw," he vowed and swore descriptively.

When she approached the door of the study, she paused, not wanting to eavesdrop on a private conversation.

"I want to know who in the hell is responsible," Trevor nearly shouted into the receiver and then waited impatiently for the person on the other end of the phone to respond. "Well it's a hell of a way to run a campaign, if you ask me.... What? Yeah, I'm not going anywhere." He looked pointedly at his watch. "See ya then."

Ashley noticed the lines of strain in the rigid set of his jaw and she remembered his look just the night before when he had seemed so beaten. Her mouth went dry when she realized that he hadn't been honest with her. There was still a secret gnawing at his insides and she knew instinctively that it had something to do with her. He looked as if he were a man possessed.

When he slammed the receiver down, his mouth was drawn into a thin, determined line. Rubbing the tension from the back of his neck and shoulders, he closed his eyes and stretched. "Damn!" he muttered, thinking he was alone.

"What happened?" Ashley asked. His eyes flew open and he turned his head in her direction.

"What hasn't?" His fingers rubbed anxiously against the heel of his hands. "Looks like Claud beat me to the punch...."

"What do you mean?"

Trevor cocked his head in the direction of the front page of the newspaper, which was lying near the phone on his desk. "See for yourself," he invited with a dark scowl.

Ashley crossed the room, reached for the paper and as her eyes scanned the headlines her stomach began to knot painfully. "Oh, my God," she whispered when she found the article about Trevor. The by-line indicated that the story had been written by Elwin Douglass, the young reporter who had accosted her at Pioneer Square just the previous afternoon. Ashley felt her knees beginning to buckle and she had to lean against the bookcase for support.

The article was a scandalous piece of yellow journalism about Trevor and his affair with the daughter of Lazarus Stephens, who was currently president of Stephens Timber Corporation. Slanted in such a manner as to present the worst possible image of Trevor, the story, which had fragmented pieces of the truth woven into a blanket of lies, suggested that Ashley and Trevor had been lovers for the past eight years, even during her brief marriage to Richard Jennings.

Ashley swallowed against the nausea rising in her throat. There were enough facts within the text of the article to make the report appear well researched. It would be blindingly obvious to any reader that someone close to the story had been interviewed.

The premise of the article was that since Trevor was so close to his own family's business, as well as entrapped in a relationship with Ashley Stephens Jennings, of Stephens Timber, he couldn't possibly support a campaign of wilderness protection and environmentalism with any modicum of sincerity in his bid for the senate.

The truth of the matter is, the article concluded, *that our would-be senator spends more time with people closely associated with business and industry than with the environmentalists who support him. Trevor Daniels seems to be able to speak out of both sides of his mouth with great ease and little conscience.*

Ashley's face had drained of color and she was trembling by the time she finished reading the condemning article. "This is all a lie," she said, shaking the crumpled paper in the air indignantly.

"You can thank dear cousin Claud for that," Trevor replied, pacing the floor.

"Dear God, I'm so sorry," Ashley whispered, lowering her head into her palm.

"For what? Being related to that bastard? You didn't have much choice in the matter."

"No, you don't understand. I don't think Claud was behind this. Yesterday, at Pioneer Square—I had gone there to look for you, and when you didn't show up, I approached Everett...."

Trevor's head snapped up to look in her direction and his dark gaze hardened. "Go on," he suggested. A cold feeling of dread was beginning to steal over him. What was Ashley admitting?

She lifted her palms in a supplicating gesture before letting them fall to her sides in defeat. "When Everett left, I began to walk back to the office and this guy, Douglass, started walking with me and began asking questions. You know: Wasn't I Ashley Jennings? Didn't I know Trevor Daniels? Was it true that I was president of Stephens Timber? That sort of thing."

"And you talked to him?" The gleam in Trevor's eye was deadly.

"No! At least I tried not to. But he wouldn't stop walking with me...kept requesting an interview." She shook her head at her own folly. "I refused, of course, only answering his questions as briefly and politely as possible. I guess I didn't want to look like a snob. Anyway, he kept asking about an interview and I told him to talk to the office and make an appointment." She shrugged her slim shoulders. "It was stupid of me."

Trevor squeezed his eyes shut tightly and rubbed his temples. "So how did this guy know you would be there?"

"He couldn't have. I didn't tell anyone."

"Not even Claud?"

"He was out of town, remember, in Seattle talking to you."

"But he must have known. Somehow. Someone at the office must have told him."

"I don't think so. I wouldn't have gone to the rally if I thought he would find out about it."

"So you don't trust him either?" Trevor cocked a questioning black brow in her direction. A guarded secret lurked in his dark gaze.

"Of course not, at least not since we found the evidence against him. And one day I walked into his office and overheard him telling someone that...well, I don't know for sure if he meant you, he never said your name, but he said, 'We can't let that son of a bitch win....' When he saw me he pretended that the conversation was about an ad campaign, but—"

"You didn't believe him?"

"No."

"Unless I miss my guess, Claud's behind all this." The doorbell rang and Trevor frowned. "That must be Everett. Watch out, he's fit to be tied."

"Aren't you going to answer it?"

Trevor shook his head. "He has a key. He just rings the bell to warn me—"

"Why?"

A sly smile slanted across Trevor's handsome face and he trailed a familiar finger along the curve of her jaw. "Just in case I'm in bed with a beautiful woman."

"Give me a break."

"I'll give you more than that." His dark eyes penetrated the sadness in her gaze. "Buck up," he suggested, squeezing her shoulders fondly. She felt the strength and determination of his character in his touch. "We'll rise above all this political dirt."

"I don't see how." As far as Ashley was concerned, everything she'd hoped for, especially a future with Trevor, was slipping away from her. "Maybe you should tell me everything. Trevor, I know that something's bothering you—"

Everett Woodward stormed into the den in a rage. His face was puckered into a belligerent scowl that darkened when he saw Ashley. He tossed his briefcase and a copy of the *Morning Surveyor* onto the couch before glaring pointedly at Trevor.

"Well, that's it—the ball game," Everett announced without the civility of a greeting. "All that work and effort right down the proverbial drain."

"Don't you think you're overreacting?" Trevor interposed with a bitter smile.

"Overreacting? *Overreacting!*" Everett retorted, his round face going beet red. "For God's sake, man, your career is on the line here, and you have the audacity to suggest that I'm—"

"Jumping off the deep end."

Everett let out a long, bewildered breath. "What're you doing here?" he asked Ashley when he turned his attention away from Trevor and trained his furious light eyes on her. "Was this Claud's idea, too?"

"That's enough, Everett," Trevor warned. "Ashley's staying here." There was a fierceness in Trevor's voice that made Ashley shudder. His fingers, which had touched her lightly on the shoulder, gripped her more savagely, as if in proof of his possession.

"You're joking!"

"Not at all. We're going to get married as soon as possible."

"Not on your life! You can't; not now! The press will have a field day with the both of you," Everett exclaimed, stunned, his eyes widening behind thick glasses. He took hold of Trevor's sleeve and looked into the candidate's eyes. "Not now, Trevor. You can't associate with Ashley or anyone else at Stephens Timber without looking like a hypocrite. You've already lost points in the most recent polls. All those rumors about withdrawing from the race really hurt you, and now this." He pointed an outraged, shaking finger at the condemning newspaper on the couch. "The last thing you can do right now is announce an engagement to the president of Stephens Timber, for Christ's sake!"

"I said we're going to get married."

Everett was thinking fast when he turned pleading eyes upon Ashley. "Can't you talk some sense into him? What would waiting another year hurt? The campaign would be over—he'd be comfortable in Washington. You could get married then."

"Forget it, Everett. I've made my decision." Trevor's voice was firm; his determination was registered in the tight muscles surrounding his mouth.

"Oh, Lord," Everett said with a sigh. He sunk into the soft cushions of the couch before swearing roundly. "I need a drink."

"It's only ten in the morning—"

"Make it a double."

Trevor smiled at the campaign manager's pale complexion. "How about champagne? To celebrate?"

"Scotch."

Trevor laughed aloud and poured the portly man a stiff drink. Everett accepted it gratefully, took a long swallow and sighed audibly. "I don't suppose you'll name your first child after me, will you?" He raised his sheepish eyes in Ashley's direction.

"We'll see," she said with a smile, relieved that the tense confrontation had abated.

"You're serious about this, aren't you?" Everett asked Trevor.

Trevor cast a meaningful smile at Ashley. "More serious than I've ever been in my life."

"Even if it means losing the election?"

"No matter what."

Again Everett let out a defeated sigh. "Well, just for the record, I think this is political suicide. You're going to alienate every voter in this state. And if you think today's article was bad, just you wait. The press will cut you to ribbons and make today's story seem like a piece of cake.

"Just for once, it would be nice if you would do things the conventional way." He looked at Trevor's thick, unruly hair, the faded jeans and the cotton shirt with the rolled-up sleeves. "But then you never do, do you?"

Trevor crossed his arms over his chest and frowned at his campaign manager and friend. "Do you want to resign?"

Everett weighed the decision. "No. At least not yet, unless you'd rather have someone else."

"Don't be ridiculous." Trevor forced a smile that was as charming as it was self-effacing. "Who else would put up with me?"

"No one in his right mind."

"Good." Trevor clasped Everett's hand. "Then everything's settled."

"I wouldn't say that." Everett wiped the accumulation of sweat that beaded his balding head. "Oh, hell. Let's go over campaign strategy, what little there is left of it."

The two men discussed politics on the leather couch in the study while Ashley poured them each a cup of coffee. After she had placed the cups on the scarred oak table, Trevor took hold of her wrist and forced her to sit next to him before asking her opinion on several issues.

Never one to withhold her opinions, Ashley pointed out what she considered flaws in the campaign, and even Everett had to grudgingly agree with some of her opinions. More than once, out of the corner of her eye, she caught Everett silently nodding encouragement to her, while she explained her feelings regarding Trevor's campaign and the issues.

Trevor smiled at her continually and attacked Everett's arguments calmly. He explained that he wasn't against the timber industry as a whole. How could he be? Daniels Logging Company was a part of his heritage. He only objected to some of the shady business practices of a few of the companies, a prime example being Stephens Timber.

"I still think you should wait to announce your engagement," Everett offered, a hopeful light showing in his eyes. "At least until after the primary. Once you're the party's candidate—"

"No dice."

"But with this article and all, it might look as if you're buckling under to bad press."

"I don't care how it looks."

"All right, all right," the campaign manager said in utter defeat. "Have it your way—you always do anyway." He snapped his briefcase closed and sighed. The round man left the house shaking his balding head.

"Maybe you should listen to him," Ashley suggested, once Everett had driven away and Trevor had closed the door to take her into his arms.

"Why start now?"

"I'm serious—"

"So am I." They were standing in the foyer of the large house. Thin shafts of wintry sunlight pierced through the long windows on either side of the door. The strong arms around her tightened.

"Look, lady, you're not weaseling out of this marriage no matter how hard you try."

"But your career—"

"Can go to hell if it means I have to knuckle under to the Claud Stephenses of the world. I'm sick and tired of worrying about how anything I do will reflect on my political image. I like to think that I learn from my mistakes, and I'm not about to repeat them. You're going to be my wife come hell or high water!"

"As if I don't have any say in the matter."

"You said plenty last night," he reminded her, kissing her tenderly on the lips. A warm rush of desire began to flow through her.

Ashley smiled and shook her head. Being in Trevor's arms made concentration on anything but his exciting touch impossible. "So what are we going to do about Claud?"

The smile that spread slowly across Trevor's face was positively sinful. He reached behind her and grabbed two coats from the curved spokes of the brass hall tree. After helping her with her down-filled garment, he slid his arms into a denim jacket.

"I doubt that we'll have to worry about Claud much longer," Trevor stated cryptically as he led her out of the front door and draped his arm over her shoulders.

"What have you done?"

"Something I should have done about six months ago. I hired a private investigator." They walked along a brick path leading around the great house toward the river. "He's been on the case for about a month, I guess."

"And that's who you were talking to last night," Ashley suddenly realized. Perhaps now he would explain everything and drive away the lingering doubts in her mind.

"Right." Trevor winked broadly. "With what this guy has found out on his own and the evidence you and John Ellis supplied, I think we'll have enough proof of Claud's illegal activities to lock him up for a while."

"If he doesn't get to you first."

"I'm not too worried about that." Taking her chilled hand in his, he led her to the banks of the silvery Willamette. The wind on the water was brisk, causing white-caps to swell on the swiftly flowing current. Trevor leaned against the trunk of a barren maple tree and placed his arms securely around her waist. She leaned against him, feeling the warmth of his body surrounding hers while the chill winter wind blew against her face.

"This isn't going to be easy for you, you know," he suggested. "Claud will make it rough. How will you feel if you have to testify against him?"

She shrugged her shoulders. "I don't know. I guess I'll have to wait and see how involved he is."

"Oh, he's involved all right. Right up to his scrawny mustache."

Ashley closed her eyes and fought against any feelings of sympathy she might harbor for her cousin. "You know there's no love lost between us. I swear that he wanted to kill me when he found out that Dad hadn't disinherited me as the rest of the family had thought. I was hoping that he would learn to live with the fact that I own the majority of shares of the corporation, but..." She sighed and shrugged her slim shoulders. "I doubt if he'll ever really accept that I'm his boss. It's hard for him, but that's no excuse for what he's put you through. I just kept him on the payroll because the company needed his expertise and because I wasn't sure that he had done everything you thought.... Now I know differently."

She felt the strain in Trevor's body and his arms circled her as if to protect her from all the evil and injustice in the world. Once again she had the feeling that there was something bothering him, a secret he was afraid to divulge. His cold lips brushed against the crook of her neck. "I think that you should leave," he cautioned.

The words hit her with the force of an arctic gale. Hadn't he just insisted that she marry him? "Leave—to go where?"

"Maybe you should go out of town, just for a couple of days. Until I get some things ironed out."

"But why?"

"Because the press is going to be all over me. And you. Everett wasn't kidding when he said that they'll put us through hell once they find out that we're going to get married. And when the story about Claud breaks—I doubt if either of us will have a minute's peace." He let out a weary gust of breath that misted in the frigid morning air. "As a matter of fact, I'll bet we get more than our share of visitors this afternoon. Everett said·that several reporters had already tried to contact me at campaign headquarters. It's just a matter of time before they show up here."

"That may be true, but I'm not leaving," Ashley decided with a proud toss of her head.

"Haven't you listened to a word I've said?" Was there a thread of desperation in his words?

"And that's why I'm staying." She turned to face him and held his square jaw between her hands. "I'm tired of running from everything, including the truth. If I'm going to marry you, and you can be sure that I am, then I'd better get used to the occupational hazards of being a senator's wife."

"If I win."

"*When* you win."

A slow-spreading smile creeped over Trevor's handsome features and the sun seemed to radiate from the midnight blue of his eyes. "You're an incredible woman," he whispered, his throat feeling uncomfortably swollen. "And I don't want to do anything that would put you in jeopardy. I can't lose you, not again."

"You won't. Hey, I've seen my share of bad press," Ashley stated, thinking of all of the gossip surrounding her father and the family business, "and I think I can handle whatever they dish out."

"I can't talk you into leaving, just for a couple of days?"

"It would be a waste of your breath and my time."

"So you intend to stay."

"Forever," she said with a sigh as his arms crushed her against him.

Trevor pressed his lips against her black hair. "You may as well know that I'm not into long engagements."

"Neither am I." She clung to him and listened to the steady, comforting beat of his heart, knowing she could face anything the future had to offer, as long as she was with the man she loved.

"Then, next month. Or sooner."

She smiled against the coarse denim of his jacket. "We have plenty of time," she whispered as tears of happiness pooled in her eyes.

Two hours later, after breakfast, the first reporter called. Trevor took the call, declined an interview, referred the reporter to Everett Woodward and slammed down the receiver.

"Well, it's started," he said, his piercing blue eyes holding her gaze. "If you want out, you better make a hasty exit."

"Not on your life."

Quickly she called Mrs. Deveraux to explain the situation, in case any reporters started looking for her. The fussy old woman burst into tears of happiness when Ashley mentioned that she and Trevor were going to be married.

"And here I was worried about you," Francine exclaimed, clucking her tongue. "I should have guessed that you never got over that man."

"It's not quite like it appears in the papers," Ashley stated, hoping to start rectifying the damage to her reputation that the *Morning Surveyor* had wrought.

"Of course it isn't. Who would believe a story like that?" Francine asked indignantly.

"No one, I hope. Look, I'll come back to the house later in the day and pick up a few of my things."

"Good. Then you can tell me all about it. Oh, I almost forgot," the housekeeper stated as an afterthought. "Your cousin has been calling this morning—"

"Claud?" Ashley asked, and Trevor, overhearing the name, whirled to face her. Every muscle on his face was pulled taut.

"He needs to talk to you."

"Isn't he still in Seattle?"

"Oh, no. He got back into town sometime last night, I think." Ashley was sure that Claud wasn't due back into town until the day after next, and from the deadly look in Trevor's eyes she felt instant dread.

"Did you tell him where I was?"

"Oh, no. I explained that you had gone shopping for the day and that I would give you his message."

"How did he take the news?"

"As usual. Not well."

"So things are normal," Ashley thought aloud, though the darkness in Trevor's eyes warned her that just the opposite was true. "I'll see you later."

After Ashley hung up, Trevor switched on the answering machine and began to pace from room to room like a caged animal, alternately surveying the telephone as if in indecision and then looking carefully out the windows to the long, asphalt drive.

"I take it that Claud's back in town," Trevor said, his hands pushing impatiently through his coarse hair.

"He's looking for me."

Trevor stopped midstride. "Damn! I knew I couldn't trust that bastard!"

Ashley put a hand on Trevor's forearm and found the muscles rigid. "What's going on?"

The telephone rang and the recorder automatically took the call. "You know, it wouldn't surprise me to find out that Claud called all the papers in town," Trevor remarked with an undertone of vengeance.

"You can't blame him for everything," Ashley replied with a frown.

Trevor took her hand and led her to the couch in the study. "I think it's about time you knew what we're up against," he said with obvious regret. "Pete Young, the private investigator I hired, looked into several things: the accident with my car, the bribery charges and—"

"Your father's disappearance," Ashley guessed with a shudder.

"Right. Now that the press is involved, it could get very unpleasant."

She smiled despite the dread inching up her spine. "I know." Settling into the corner cushions, Ashley tucked her feet beneath her and stared up at Trevor as he paced the floor.

"When I talked to Pete last night, he was sure that he had enough evidence to prove that Claud had paid to have my car tampered with. He found someone at the garage where my car was serviced who was willing to talk, for a small fee."

"So Claud paid off a mechanic to tamper with your car." Ashley felt sick inside, as if a part of her were slowly dying. She had thought her cousin capable of deceit, and bribery perhaps, but something this cold-blooded and cruel was beyond those bounds. "Dear God," she whispered, turning cold inside.

The corners around Trevor's mouth pulled downward. "According to Everett, Pete also thinks that Claud planted the story in the paper."

"But the reporter talked to me," Ashley offered tonelessly. Why was she even trying to defend her cousin?

"Because somehow he knew that you would be there, or maybe it was just a lucky guess on his part. It doesn't matter. I'll bet that Claud was involved."

Ashley lowered her forehead into her hands and gave in to the tears threatening her eyes. "I really didn't think it would all come down to this," she whispered. All the lies about her family and her father were really true.

Trevor sat on the couch beside her and kissed away the lines etching her smooth brow. "We can handle it if we just stick together."

"I thought you wanted me to leave."

He took her hand and his eyes narrowed in concern. "I never want you to leave, but I think that it might be safer for you."

"Safer?" Her face suddenly lost all expression as the meaning of his words became clear and rang dully in her weary mind. "There's something you haven't been telling me, isn't there? A reason why you want me to go. Ever since I got here last night, I've had the feeling that there was something bothering you, as if there is some kind of danger lurking around every corner. It's more than concern about your reputation or even losing the senatorial race, isn't it?

"Trevor, what's going on? And don't give me any double talk about reporters and mudslinging." Her face was grave. "I want the truth. All of it. And I want it now."

Trevor let out a weary sigh and touched her cheek tenderly before lowering his eyes.

"What did Claud say, Trevor? When I came here last night you said something to the effect that you never thought you'd see me again. At the time, I thought you were talking about the scandal, but it's more than that, isn't it?" She noticed him wince and pale and a wave of understanding washed over her in cold rushes of the truth. Everything, all of Trevor's actions, were beginning to make sense. "Oh my God...Claud threatened you, didn't he? *And...the price was my life!*"

Chapter Twelve

Trevor closed his eyes against the cold truth. His lips whitened and he swallowed back the savage rage that had been with him for the better part of two days.

"Yes," he ground out, as if the admission itself were tearing him into small pieces, making him impotent against the injustice of the world. "Claud told me point-blank that if I didn't get out of the race, you would get hurt."

"But he only meant that he would ruin my reputation," Ashley protested weakly.

Trevor's eyes glittered dangerously. "He meant that and more. He'd feed you to the wolves if it would save his skin."

"But surely you couldn't believe—"

"What I couldn't do was take a chance with your life. I know how ruthless your cousin can be. He nearly killed me by having my car tampered with, and I'll lay you odds that he was involved in my father's disappearance."

"But he was only twenty-two."

"And a very ruthless, determined man. He learned his lessons from the master well."

"Meaning my father." Ashley slumped against the cushions of the couch, wishing there was some way to end the pain, the agony, the bitterness and hatred between the families of Stephens and Daniels.

"Are you beginning to understand what we're facing?" he asked. "That's why I think you should go away. Just until Claud is safely behind bars and the press has cooled off a little."

Ashley shook her head. "It won't matter. If I did leave, the minute I'd get back to Portland, someone would hear about it and the reporters would start to track me down. That's how it works. If I left we'd only be putting off the inevitable. As for Claud, I'm not afraid of him. I told you before that violence isn't his style. If there's dirty work to be done, he'd hire someone else to do it, and I can't really believe that he's desperate enough to harm me.

"I'm staying and we're going to fight this thing together," she finished determinedly. A small, proud smile touched Trevor's lips. Having made her decision, she straightened, slipped on her shoes and stood.

Trevor was still considering the options. She noticed that the wariness hadn't left his eyes. "Then you're staying here, with me. That way, I'll know you're safe."

"I can't just sit around here like some fearful hostage. I've got a job—"

"With Claud."

"That will be rectified very shortly."

"Then stay with me for a couple of days—"

"Just that long?"

Trevor smiled despite his fears. "You're welcome forever, you know that. As far as going to work, forget it. You'd be too vulnerable."

"I can't—"

"Let that accountant take care of things."

"For how long?"

"As long as it takes for the private investigator to put the pieces together and convince the police that Claud's dangerous."

"Oh, Trevor, you're jumping at shadows. Claud would never hurt me."

"That's a chance I'm not willing to take."

Seeing that there was no way she could convince him otherwise, she gave in. "In that case, I'd better dash home and pack a few things."

"I think it would be safer if you stayed here."

Ashley smiled indulgently. "I've lived in these clothes for two days. I need to change into something more practical than heels, a silk blouse and a skirt. I feel positively grody."

Trevor's eyes slid down her body. "You look great."

"But I feel sticky. Now, nothing you have here is going to fit, so I'd better go home and pack a few things. I'll be perfectly safe. Mrs. Deveraux is home; I just called her a few minutes ago."

"I don't know—"

"Give me a break, Trevor."

"All right. I'll come with you," he said finally, reaching for his wallet and stuffing it into his back pocket.

"I thought you had to stay here and wait for Everett's call."

"The recorder will take the message. Or, he'll call back."

"But—"

"You're stuck with me, okay? I've worried enough about you and I'm not about to let you out of my sight, not until I'm satisfied that you're not in any danger."

"Worrywart."

Trevor helped her with her coat and his fingers lingered on the back of her neck. "It's just that I can't take any chances," he said roughly, his voice catching on the words. "You're the most important thing in my life." Gently he touched her shoulders, forcing her to turn and face him. "Nothing else matters—my career, this house—" he gestured widely to encompass all of the estate "—nothing. Unless you're with me."

"But for so many years—"

"I was alone. I lived, Ashley, and I thought I could bury myself in my work. I guess I was somewhat satisfied. But then in December, when I saw you again, I knew that I'd been living a lie and that I could never go back to that empty life again."

"But you didn't call, or write. I didn't hear anything from you."

"Because I knew that it would be no good until we settled what had happened in the past. And that included the truth about your family as well as mine."

Just as Trevor reached for the handle of the door, Ashley heard a car roar down the driveway.

"Damn," Trevor muttered. "Too late. Some reporter must have gotten tired of leaving a message with the recorder." His blue eyes pierced into hers. "Are you ready for this?"

Ashley braced herself and her fingers twined in the strength of his. "As ready as I'll ever be."

The doorbell rang impatiently several times and then a fist pounded furiously on the door.

"Not the most patient guy around," Trevor mumbled. "I've got a bad feeling about this."

He jerked open the door and Claud rushed into the foyer, his face ashen, his eyes dark with accusations when they rested on Ashley.

"Wait a minute," Trevor said, placing his body between that of Ashley and her cousin. "What're you doing here?"

"We had a deal," Claud spat out. Then he straightened, regained a small portion of his dignity and let his cold eyes rest on Ashley. "I thought I'd find you here."

"What do you want, Claud?"

"Call him off!" her cousin blurted furiously.

"Who? What?"

"Him!" Claud pointed an accusatory finger in Trevor's direction and it shook with the rage enveloping him. "That bastard's been hounding me for the last month."

"I think you should calm down—"

"And *I* think you should leave, while you still can." Trevor's eyes snapped.

Claud stopped abruptly. "What's that supposed to mean?"

"Just that we're on to you, Stephens."

Visibly paling, Claud turned to Ashley. "He's been telling you all sorts of lies, I suppose."

Ashley held out her palm, hoping to diffuse the uncomfortable tension. She never really had been afraid of her cousin and she couldn't really fear him now. Despite Trevor's accusations, Claud was too much of a coward to try to do her physical harm. "Why don't we all go into the living room and I'll make some coffee. We can discuss whatever it is we need to, once everyone has calmed down."

"I don't know...." Trevor said, his eyes calculating as he studied his opponent.

"I don't want any coffee—"

"Something stronger?" Ashley asked, watching Claud walk agitatedly back and forth in the foyer. She started toward the living room and Claud followed.

"I need to talk to you alone."

"Not on your life," Trevor boomed, falling into step with Ashley. "I'm not about to forget what you said a couple of days ago, something to the effect that Ashley was expendable and you were willing to do the expending."

"He's lying, Ash! I swear—"

"Don't waste your breath," Trevor suggested, and the look of steely determination in his eyes coupled with his tightly clenched fists convinced Claud to keep quiet.

Claud sank into one of the stiff royal blue chairs near the bay window and had to hold on to his knee to keep it from shaking. "There's been some guy following me, Ashley," he said, avoiding the deadly look on Trevor's face and concentrating on his cousin. "I don't know who or why, but I think that it's someone looking for information about the company. You know, there's kidnappings all the time—families with money."

"Don't flatter yourself," Trevor said with a cynical smile growing from one side of his face to the other. He sat next to Ashley on the couch, one arm curved protectively over her shoulders, the other at his side. He looked coolly disinterested, almost bored with the conversation, but he was tense, all of his muscles coiled. Ashley could feel it. If he had to, Trevor was ready to spring on Claud.

"I think someone might try to kidnap me, for God's sake!"

"Why? Who would pay the ransom?" Trevor demanded, his lips curling bitterly.

"Ashley, please. Can I talk to you alone?" Claud was beginning to sweat. Tiny droplets formed on his forehead and there was a note of desperation in his voice.

"Forget it."

"I can speak for myself," Ashley intervened, but Trevor would hear none of it. He leaned forward, pushing his body closer and more threateningly toward Claud.

"While we're on the subject of kidnappings, why don't we discuss what happened to my father," Trevor suggested, his voice low and demanding. "I have an idea that you know just what went on ten years ago."

Claud lost all his color. His bravado was dismantled and he suddenly looked like a very small and frightened man. Nervously, he toyed with his mustache.

Movement caught Trevor's eye and he looked from the scared face of Ashley's cousin through the window behind Claud. "It looks as if we have more company—"

"What?" Claud's gaze moved to the long drive and he saw the police car driving toward the house. "Oh my God..." Turning frantic eyes on Ashley, he whispered, "You can't let this happen. Daniels is trying to frame me for something that I had no part in. Ashley—for God's sake, you're my cousin, can't you help me?"

Ashley's throat was dry. No matter how miserable Claud was, he was still her own flesh and blood. The doorbell rang impatiently just as she answered. "I'll call Nick Simpson."

"Jesus Christ, Ash, I need more than an attorney!"

"Then I suggest you start talking, and fast," Trevor insisted, "if you want to save your miserable hide."

Trevor was convinced that Claud wouldn't do anything harmful to the one person he felt would save him. "Stay where you are," he warned as he left to answer the door.

Claud nearly leaped across the living room, so that he was close to Ashley. "I need to get out of here. I just want a little time, show me the back way out—"

"You can't escape like they do on TV, Claud. This isn't 'Magnum, P.I.'"

"But I haven't done anything—"

His words were cut off by the entrance of two policemen.

"Claud Stephens?" the taller of the two asked.

Claud made one more appealing look in Ashley's direction before straightening and finally finding his voice. "Yes?"

As Ashley sat in stunned disbelief, the officer read Claud his rights and escorted him outside to the waiting police car. For several minutes she sat on the couch, trying to quell the storm of emotions raging within her.

"Was that really necessary?" she asked, her eyes searching the harsh angles of Trevor's face once he returned to the living room.

"I wish it weren't," he admitted, "but whether you believe it or not, Claud can be dangerous." He noticed that Ashley had paled. She was still wearing her coat, but looked as if she were cold and dead inside.

"I don't think we should go anywhere, not for a while." He came back to the couch and wrapped comforting arms around her. "Come on," he said, squeezing her tightly, "I'll get you a drink."

"I...I don't think I want one."

"It's been a rough couple of days, and it's bound to get worse," he cajoled.

"Then I think I'd better keep my wits about me." She ran her anxious fingers through her blue-black hair. "And there's no reason to put off going back to the house, now that the police have Claud." She forced her uneasiness aside and tried to concentrate on Trevor and her love for him. Regardless of anything that might come between them in the future, she felt secure in his love.

"I don't think it would be wise—"

Ashley placed a steady finger to his lips. "Shhh. If I'm going to be your wife, Senator, I'd better learn to cope with crises, wouldn't you say?"

"It's going to get worse before it gets better."

"But that's what it's all about, isn't it—for better or for worse?"

"You are incredible," he said with a seductive smile.

She slapped him on the thigh and stood up, filled with renewed conviction. "Let's get a move on. I wouldn't want to miss the reporters when they get here."

Trevor groaned, but got off of the couch. "Anything you say." He laughed and kissed her lightly on the forehead.

When they returned to Trevor's home, after having tea and a lengthy discussion with Mrs. Deveraux, Trevor checked the messages on the tape recorder. As he had suspected, several reporters had called requesting interviews. There was also a terse message from Everett to call him immediately.

Trevor dialed Everett's number and smiled wickedly as the agitated campaign manager answered.

"I thought you were going to wait for my call," Everett complained. Trevor could picture steam coming out of the campaign manager's ears.

"I had other things on my mind...." Trevor's eyes slid appreciatively up Ashley's body. Dressed in jeans and a red sweater, with her black hair looped into a loose braid wound at the base of her neck, she looked comfortable and at home in Trevor's huge house.

"I'll bet," Everett replied. "Now that you and Ashley are together, you'll never be able to keep your mind on the campaign."

"That would be a shame," Trevor murmured irreverently as his eyes followed Ashley up the polished wooden stairs. She was carrying two suitcases, oblivious to his stare or the fact that her jeans were stretched provocatively over her behind as she mounted each step.

"Listen, there are a couple of things you really should know," Everett commanded. "And they have to do with Ashley and Stephens Timber."

The low tone of Everett's voice and the mention of Ashley's name captured Trevor's attention. "I'm listening."

"You'd better brace yourself," Everett warned. "Claud Stephens has started to talk...."

Ashley felt his eyes on her back as she unfolded the last blouse and hung it in the closet. She whirled to face Trevor, a sly smile perched on her lips. "What took you so long?" she asked, but the wicked grin fell from her face when she saw Trevor's expression. He was leaning against the doorframe, watching her silently and fighting the overwhelming urge to break down. "What happened?"

She was beside him in an instant, placing her warm hands against his face. He managed a bitter smile filled with grief.

"The case against Claud looks pretty solid," Trevor said at length, while gazing into the misty depths of her sea-green eyes. "The private investigator I hired called Everett when he couldn't reach me."

"And?"

"Claud's having a rough time. He can't seem to make up his mind whether he needs an attorney or should plea-bargain on his own. I think he opted for the lawyer."

"I hope so," Ashley said fervently. "Claud's used to doing things his own way, and since he's a lawyer I was afraid he would try to defend himself."

"He's smarter than that." Trevor entered the room and sat down on the edge of the bed. His shoulders sagged and he forced tense fingers through his unruly chestnut hair.

"What else?" Ashley asked as she sat next to him. She felt her throat constrict with dread. Something horrible had happened to Trevor. *What?*

Trevor's midnight-blue eyes pierced into hers and his arms wrapped around her as if in support. "Claud's desperately trying to clear his own name, you realize."

"And?"

"And he's saying that Lazarus is the one who insti- gated the bribery charges against me last summer as well as having kidnapped my father ten years ago."

Ashley felt as if a hot knife had been driven into her heart. She slumped for a minute, but Trevor's strong arms gripped her. "It's not unexpected," she said, her voice failing her. "It's just that I hoped and prayed that Dad wasn't involved." She let out a long breath of air and realized that she had to know everything before she could start her life with Trevor.

"What happened?"

"Claud's saying that my father had gained informa- tion proving that Lazarus had used the harmful pesticide near Springfield—the one that's subsequently been linked to the deaths."

"I remember." Ashley fought against the sick feeling deep within her. Dennis Lange had been a friend of Trevor's and had died because of her father's neglect. His was just one of several families who had been inadvertently poisoned by the spraying.

"Claud seems to think that Lazarus knew what the impact of the spraying would be and the hazards it would impose on the residents as well as the environment. Lazarus panicked when he found out that my father was meeting with the lobbyist in Washington, and after the meeting, he coerced him into his car. They drove to your father's cabin—"

"No!" Not the place where she and Trevor had made love. "Not the cabin."

Trevor's hold on her shoulders increased. "Lazarus tried to buy my father's silence, and an argument ensued. Dad tried to escape from the cabin and he fell down an embankment, probably breaking his neck. Lazarus was afraid that he would be up on kidnapping, bribery and probably negligent homicide charges, so he buried my father somewhere on his land in the Cascades."

"Oh dear God," Ashley murmured, seeing the bitterness in Trevor's features. "Trevor... I'm so sorry, so sorry," she murmured, releasing the hot tears that had burned behind her eyelids and letting them trickle slowly down her face.

"It's not your fault—"

"But I never believed—I couldn't face it."

Gathering strength from the warmth of her body, Trevor let out a long, trembling sigh. "I knew Dad was dead, you know. I just kept hoping that I'd been wrong, that someday he'd show up again. But deep in my heart, I knew."

The news was too distressing for Ashley. She extricated herself from Trevor's embrace, walked across the room and stared out the window to the clear, ever-changing waters of the Willamette River.

"I knew that my father wasn't a warm person. And I might have even gone so far as to say that he was unthinking and therefore unkind. But I never thought of him as cruel or ruthless." She shook her head and let the tears of pain slide down her cheeks. "There's not much I can do except make a settlement with those poor victims in Springfield. It won't bring back the dead, but maybe it will help their children." Her shoulders stiffened with newfound pride. "And I'll make sure that Stephens Timber Corporation complies with every government and environmental standard as long as I'm involved," she promised.

When she walked back toward the bed, Trevor was staring at her, admiring her strength. He captured her wrist and pulled her down on the bed with him before offering kisses born of sorrow and grief.

"Don't ever leave me," he begged.

"Never...oh, darling." She kissed him with all the fervor her torn emotions could provide. "It's all behind us now."

The telephone rang and Trevor eyed it with disgust. "Go away," he muttered.

"It's the private line. You'd better answer it."

"It could be more bad news."

She smiled through the sheen of her tears. "Then we'll face it together." Hastily brushing her tears aside, she curled against him, feeling more loved and protected than ever.

He frowned and answered the intrusive instrument.

"You and that damned recording machine!" Everett blasted. "I hate talking to those things. I just thought I'd better warn you, the press has gotten hold of Claud's story."

"I expected as much."

"Bill Orson is in a near-panic. You know he was pretty tight with Claud and the rest of the timber industry. Orson has already begun amending his stand on the environment and it looks to me that despite everything, you still have a good chance of winning the election. Orson's been in too tight with Claud Stephens to come out clean on this one."

"Good."

There was a stilted silence in the conversation. "You're still in the running, aren't you?" Everett asked.

"I'll let you know tomorrow...or maybe next week," Trevor replied, looking meaningfully at Ashley. "Right now I'm busy, Everett."

"What the devil?"

"How would you like to be best man at my wedding?"

"Today?"

Trevor laughed aloud. "Very soon, Everett, very soon." With his final words, he dropped the phone and took Ashley into his arms.

"Everett's not going to appreciate being treated like that," she teased.

"I don't give a damn what Everett appreciates." Slowly he removed the pins holding her hair at the nape of her neck. "Right now there's only one person I intend to satisfy."

"Your constituents wouldn't like to hear that kind of talk, Senator," she quipped.

"Oh, I don't know...I think it would improve my image if I were to become a happily married man."

"So this is just for the sake of the voters?"

"One in particular—she's very independent, you see." He unclasped the top button of her blouse. "But that may change once she's saddled with a husband and a family."

"A child?" Ashley asked, her breathing becoming irregular.

"Or two...or three." As he counted, he undid the buttons of her blouse and kissed the white skin at the base of her throat. Ashley's heart began to swell in her chest at the thought of becoming Trevor's wife and bearing his children.

"You're very persuasive, you know," she whispered.

"Years of practice, darling."

She smiled up at the man she loved. "Do you think this will ever work for us?" she asked. "There's been so much keeping us apart."

"All in the past," he assured her. "I told you I was never going to let go of you again, and I meant it." He touched the soft slope of her cheek. ''Believe me when I tell you that I love you.''

"Oh, I do, Trevor,'' she said with a sigh. She wound her arms around his neck, never to let go.

READERS' COMMENTS ON SILHOUETTE SPECIAL EDITIONS:

READERS' COMMENTS ON SILHOUETTE DESIRES

"Thank you for Silhouette Desires. They are the best thing that has happened to the bookshelves in a long time."
— V.W.*, Knoxville, TN

"Silhouette Desires—wonderful, fantastic—the best romance around."
— H.T.*, Margate, N.J.

"As a writer as well as a reader of romantic fiction, I found DESIREs most refreshingly realistic—and definitely as magical as the love captured on their pages."
— C.M.*, Silver Lake, N.Y.

"I just wanted to let you know how very much I enjoy your Silhouette Desire books. I read other romances, and I must say your books rate up at the top of the list."
— C.N.*, Anaheim, CA

"Desires are number one. I especially enjoy the endings because they just don't leave you with a kiss or embrace; they finish the story. Thank you for giving me such reading pleasure."
— M.S.*, Sandford, FL

*names available on request

Lilly

Silhouette Special Edition

COMING NEXT MONTH

THE HEART'S YEARNING—Ginna Gray
When Laura's search for the son she'd had to give up finally ended, she was content to watch him from afar...until Adam Kincaid, her son's adoptive father, unwittingly drew her into a triangle of love.

STAR-CROSSED—Ruth Langan
Fiercely protective Adam London was determined to stop B.J. Conover from writing his mother's biography, but B.J. had a job to do and she couldn't let her growing feelings for Adam stand in her way.

A PERFECT VISION—Monica Barrie
Architect Lea Graham envisioned a community nestled in the New Mexican landscape that Darren Laird was determined to preserve. Could the love that they shared survive a fight to the finish to save their separate dreams?

MEMORIES OF THE HEART—Jean Kent
Was it really possible that foundling Suzy Yoder was the long-lost Hepburn baby, heiress to a vast fortune? Attorney Rich Link had to find the answer, for reasons both legal and personal.

AUTUMN RECKONING—Maggi Charles
Deep in the Berkshire mountains, Marc Bouchard fell in love. Children's-book author Jennifer Bently was more than she'd led him to believe, and her deception threatened the love that they had dared to share.

ODDS AGAINST TOMORROW—Patti Beckman
Every jockey dreams of winning the Kentucky Derby, but for jockey Nikki Cameron the stakes were almost too high. If she triumphed on the bluegrass track, she risked losing the only man she'd ever loved.
